FIREBALL

ALAN SPENCER

SEVERED PRESS
HOBART TASMANIA

FIREBALL

WWW.SEVEREDPRESS.COM

This novel is a work of fiction. Names,
characters, places and incidents are the product of
the author's imagination, or are used fictitiously.
Any resemblance to actual events, locales or persons,
living or dead, is purely coincidental.

ISBN: 978-1-925597-05-9

PART ONE: FIREBALL STRIKES

FIERY BIRTH

Mark Avery wanted three things out of his trip to Hawaii.

Surf, sun, and sex.

What he got?

Lava, lava, and more lava.

"Keep telling yourself it's a free business trip," Ben William's, Mark's best friend and co-worker, insisted. "All expenses paid. I'm talking about food and lodging and as much booze your liver can take. Once the business part of it is over, then it's just a vacation. You'll sit through those boring timeshare meetings. That part sucks. It's not like you need them. You're an ace at selling timeshares. You're 'Mark the Shark' when it comes to selling people crap they don't want.

"Imagine it. You hit the beach, you show off your rockin' bod, and you chase some tail. I know how many hours you spend at the gym. I bet you pump iron in your sleep. You deserve some pay off for all those pushups you do. You're twenty-nine, single, and unencumbered. You're bound to get laid. This is Hawaii, after all. You know what they say. You get laid in Hawaii. Am I right?"

Ben Williams argued hard for Mark to attend the annual sales conference at Waikiki Beach. The man simply wouldn't take no for an answer. Ben eventually gave in.

Attending the conference would cost them their lives.

"I don't want to go alone, Mark. It's a long flight. The other guys from Johnson Reed, Schuman & Royce, and the mega pricks at Harbor House are all assholes. There's not enough alcohol in the world to have a good time when you have to hob knob with those butt-kissing, brown-nosing, tight-assed bores. Their anuses have God knows what stuck up in them. There's no dislodging what's in there. No scientist could come up with the proper instrument.

"Besides, those cronies would chase off all the beach bunnies. The hula skirts would hula away from us. But with you, Mark, you have this glow. It'll rub off on me, and I'll look good too. We'll both draw in the babes. They won't be able to resist us.

"We can even make up cover stories. We're not timeshares salesman. We sell organic goods. Or how about marijuana? Yeah, yeah, yeah. That's better. We run ganja from coast to coast. Women love danger. They'll be all over us. It'll rain pussy."

That won Ben over, though it wouldn't rain pussy.

It would rain something else altogether.

The National Time Share Convention turned out to be exactly how he expected. Five days of onerous meetings, talks, speeches, and team-building seminars. After the work part was done, they finally had three whole days to enjoy Waikiki Beach.

Being their first afternoon of freedom, Mark donned a pair of swim trunks, rented a surfboard, and rode some ferocious waves. The ocean smell, the cold water, the thrill of riding the waves, it worked to rid himself of the hard five days that came before this glorious moment.

Ben remained on the beach, laying on a towel asleep. He was working off a serious hangover. Mark knew when enough was enough. Ben did not.

There was no warning when hell touched down.

Most would expect the earth to rumble and the ground to quake, for something to warn of impending danger. He saw it happen with his own eyes while surfing.

From a higher elevation, there was a wide view of Diamond Head, a tuff cone volcano. The long-dormant volcano was a bursting cannon of red-hot lava. Brilliant red vomited from the hot depths.

BOOM!

BOOM!

BA-DOOM!

Explosions and concussions. Lava spewed from the giant mass. The wall of smoldering, smoking, boiling hot orange was trailing downhill towards the city of Waikiki. Anything the orange touched instantly became enveloped in flames. Both commercial and residential areas were a sitting duck for devastation.

Now, the earth was really starting to quake. He imagined tectonic plates not only scraping against each other, but being smashed, pulverized, and stomped on. Wilder waves were created by the seismic disturbances. He was having to do everything in his surfing experience to remain above water.

Meanwhile, he had a terrible view of the lava's carnage.

Ben, and the entire beach, was a boiling brew of cooking bodies. Ben's upper half was above the lava. He was waving at Mark, screaming for help as he was disintegrating into the molten red. Once his friend toppled forward, his body went *poof*, and gone! No sign of him having ever existed. People fled the lava only to discover their feet were melting at the ankles. Once they saw their feet turn to vapor, they tripped forward and fell into the mess. Left and right, bodies were succumbing to death.

Mark caught the cronies in suits sitting at the island bar in the swimming pool wetting their whistles one moment, and the next, the lava tide crashed into them. Flesh and muscle vanished to reveal white bones. The sight of a screaming man's skull was forever etched into his memory.

Then the fast force of the magma tide broke the business cronies into pieces and liquefied their remains. Hundreds of floating corpses spread about the island, literally being eaten up by steam and heat. He imagined sugar disintegrating into water. This time, the sugar was skin, the water, insane lava.

Large trenches in the earth forked and spread across the city, unleashing more of the deadly orange rancor up to the surface. The ground broke up with spreading and deepening rifts. The huddle of skyscrapers facing the Pacific Ocean were knocked off their foundations by the incoming lava's rage.

Buildings crashed against buildings, toppling over like architectural dominos. Cars in traffic would go up into smoke the second the insane lava touched steel. Police cars sank into the earth, dropping into the orange hot pools of hell. Victims in their cars literally boiled right before they evaporated.

Molten hot magma burning at 1600° C was spewing from the newly formed cracks about the city. The center of the island seemed to be lifting upwards instead of sinking. He imagined the ground having a giant's humpback. Red-hot magma flowed like blood from wounds across the top of that hump.

Was something trying to burst up from the ground?

He could only surf and watch, taking in the stink of burned flesh and the pealing screams of agony. He was thanking God when the entire island seemed to go quiet.

None of it made sense.

Wouldn't there be warnings on the news of an incoming volcano eruption? They had ways of determining when this would happen. And since when did volcano eruptions go from inside of an actual volcano to spewing up from the earth randomly like crude oil?

He focused on the rising humpback area of earth again. The area trembled and bulged. The protrusion covered a mile in each direction. Was the island about to blow like a ticking time bomb?

A new realization struck him. The water wasn't so cold anymore. The ocean around the island was boiling and bubbling. He was being cooked himself.

He surfed to get away from the island. The boiling had to stop somewhere, he reasoned. He wasn't getting very far. His feet were cooked so much they were active with sores. The skin was starting to slough off and reveal sections of muscle tissue.

While this was happening, the island was a puzzle breaking into pieces. Rising up from the center, a giant section of earth burst. Lava sprayed forth. Surging up from the earth was an unbelievable creature.

Mark couldn't believe it.

No way in hell, he kept thinking.

Something made sense up against his disbelief.

This wasn't a volcano erupting. Nobody could predict the occurrence, because this wasn't a weather pattern. This was birth.

The rising of the monster was the disturbance.

The monster's flesh was literally burning like flames. Lava dripped from its burning cinder-red body constantly, spattering the waters and instantly cooling off and turning into rocks.

He imagined taking a lizard's slender body and attaching the long neck of an ancient dragon, and that only began to describe its horrible magnificence.

Those blood red eyes cased the island for other life to destroy. Its primordial gaze stopped on Mark.

Out from its body spread orange wings made of sharp bone and stretched snare drum skin. From tear-duct like openings spread out along those wings sprayed flames. It was like napalm blasting from war planes. The flames cased the rest of the island. They burned so hot and fast, Mark didn't have a chance to process his demise.

He evaporated into nothing.

The island was a scorched black war zone.

The giant hole Fireball had escaped from still kicked up smoke and burbled lava.

Fireball was now airborne. It sensed no threats here. Everything was decimated.

The beast still didn't feel safe. There was something out there that sensed its existence and wanted to challenge it. Fireball followed the scent of the threat and went on the attack.

FISH SUCK

"Mary hiked a football to Moses. What in God's name am I looking at?"

Darrel Burge had woken up from an alcohol-induced sleep. When he got up to take a piss off the side of his pleasure boat, he couldn't believe what he was witnessing.

He lived on the Hawaii coastline. He often ventured out into the ocean for some peace and quiet. He retired from lathe working almost two decades ago. He was seventy-two and still kicking. His hearing wasn't so great, and his bladder couldn't hold liquor like it used to, but his eyes worked perfectly.

The ocean bubbled along the coastline for a mile in every direction. There was a suction disturbing the waters. Suction was the right word. How else to describe it?

There was a wall of sharks floating in the air, among smaller fish, and even a whale battered its body to escape—*what*? Hundreds and hundreds of marine animals were suspended in the air as if being beamed up to a spaceship.

Was something trying to empty the ocean of its life?

Darrell grabbed his binoculars. When he set his sights at what was so high up, he could barely see it. A giant burning shape. The thing that hovered in the air, batting its gnarly wings, was a brilliant red color.

It looked like a weird dragon.

Looking harder, he saw its belly was wide open. He imagined a sideways mouth. The fish were hoisted thousands of feet in the air. Giant sharks were helpless against the mysterious pull.

The stomach-mouth kept chomping, chewing, and reducing the ocean's population into digestible matter.

He stumbled and fell backwards by an invisible force.

"What the—?"

Darrell's shoes were ripped from his feet. The socks came next. Invisible hands seemed to remove them. The hairs on his head and arms bent at a strange angle, bending in the direction of the suction.

"Oh God no!"

He gripped a metal bar for his very life. His legs were above his head. He squeezed harder on the pole.

That thing ain't eating me!

The old man's convictions meant little. He wouldn't be able to hold much longer. Before he could think through his dilemma, the suction tripled in power.

His arms stayed clamped on the pole. The rest of his body flew up into the air. The break of bone and tear of sinew caused instant agony. He gasped at the sight of his bodiless arms clamped onto the pole.

He was spinning and gaining elevation.

Darrell was getting closer to the hungry belly-mouth of the beast. Before he reached high enough to view Fireball up close, his arms had come undone from the pole. They shot up with such force and speed that they collided into Darrell's skull and killed him instantly.

The ocean went still. Fireball's belly closed. The gummed-up slit drooled with digestive juices and freshly spilled blood. The prehistoric anomaly was full. Sated, the beast had one other need to be met.

Destruction.

Carnage.

Fiery infernos.

The beast spread out its leathery wings and turned its massive mega-ton body in the direction of the California coastline.

CHARGERS MASSACRE

Qualcomm Stadium was on their feet for their football team. The crowd cheered the home team as Philip Rivers lead the Chargers to yet another wild touchdown. Rivers' pass was a thirty-nine-yard floater. They were stomping their rival, the Raiders, 21-3. The Chargers' offense was shredding the opponent's defense.

The Raiders had the ball and snapped. The play started. Offense and defense clashed. Before the ball was thrown, every player on the field was bathed in flames. The players looked like the cherry of a cigarette after someone took a pull on it. A hard wind blew across them. Their bodies were so instantly cooked through that their ash remains spread like snow.

The field was ablaze. The arcs of fire spread into the stands. The scoreboard and instant replay screen erupted into multiple explosions. The crowd panicked.

One of the Chargers fans, Lisa Hemple, took in the sight. The monster hovered above the stadium. She ducked for cover.

The dragon's long, plated neck bulged in the shape of a giant ball.

A worker screaming out, "I got your hot dogs here. Hot dogs. Hot—*whaaaaaaaaaah*!" He was blanketed in flames so potent and fiery hot that the man combusted. The man's insides were molten hot and acted as bullets as they penetrated scampering people all around him. Lisa never thought she'd ever see something as insane as a burning liver cut a man's head in two halves.

Fireball was circling above. It raked its enormous black claws into the stands. It reaped fountains of blood as the incredibly sharp talons dismembered, beheaded, and disemboweled hundreds of football fans in seconds. The stands were wet with streaming tides of red.

Lisa ran for cover, tripping over a rolling head.

Her leg was caught on a long pair of intestines that hooked around her feet. Those intestines were wrapped around a pole. She couldn't get loose.

"*Nooooooooo!*"

The dragon's talon split her from pelvis to the crown of her skull.

HARD DECISIONS

"Mr. President, we need you to sign an Executive Order."

President Ted Yearling was nursing a sweating glass of bourbon in one hand and playing with a pen in the other. He was stressed sitting at his desk in the Oval Office. He heard the reports. He had very good reason to be freaking out.

Wineries in California were reduced to smoldering ash piles. Yellowstone National Park was no more. Ten cities were ablaze as he sat in the cool air conditioning of his office. Wildfires in California were a problem before, but now the wildfires were as big as towns and cities. The walls of fire were eating up everything in sight. California would be one smoldering nothing if he didn't intervene soon.

But how?

He was already sending every form of aid to help put out the fires and rescue those stranded in the flames. The body count was already high. The events promised alarming death tolls that would reach thousands. And the Chargers game. Jesus, he thought, the events were captured live on TV up to the point the whole stadium turned into a burning inferno.

The culprit was the real problem.

"Fireball" the media dubbed the flying dragon. The monster was very real. Pictures of it were spreading on the Internet. Conspiracy theorists were already chiming in as well religious crackpots claiming this was the End of Days.

Vice President, Gary Botts, was standing there impatiently. "Well, sir? We need to make decisions. The time for hesitation has passed. The nation needs your strength."

"Strength. *Hah*. Skip the rhetoric, please. What's the order? Give me the condensed version."

"The Joint Chiefs of Staff recommend we use every resource possible. The Secretary of Defense agrees. You give the Secretary of Defense complete operational command authority. They promise no tricks. They'll stop Fireball in his tracks. No more killings. We'll put the fire out and fast."

"Shouldn't we think on this more? Make a plan of attack that I can approve first?"

"Sir, if you've forgotten, your approval ratings have gone down. Ever since the scandal involving that stripper, and the pictures on Twitter—"

"Say no more! Shut up about it. I get your point. I'm a publicity nightmare. Even my dog can't look me in the eye anymore. *Sheesh.*"

"Then you understand. We need this cleaned up fast. It's a public image improvement slam dunk. If you want to be re-elected, you'll take out this dragon and fast. You save the day, the voters will say yes to the Yearling-Botts ticket come next election. You slay this dragon, there's nothing we can't accomplish. That's what the voters will think."

"Okay. Fine. I want that Goddamn lizard guy dead. I don't want him studied or dissected. I want it to be ashes. You got me?

"No. I changed my mind. I want his blood. Blow him up. Chop him up. Behead him. I don't give a damn. I want pictures on my desk by the end of the day of this creature dead. Fireball will be no more. You got me? Video tape it so we can show it off. Yeah, let's brag a little. Our military kicks ass."

The vice president handed him the piece of paper that would give full military authority to the Joint Chiefs of Staff. "Sign on the dotted line, sir."

Ted Yearling signed the document and prayed to God in the same breath.

General Sharp got the call minutes after President Yearling gave him and the Joint Chiefs of Staff full authority to take out Fireball. The general was already on the phone sending fleet after fleet of American firepower and muscle onto Fireball's ass. It didn't take more than five minutes to have a full attack assault unleashed upon the strangest adversary America had ever faced.

PROPANE BONANZA

Chuck Brundage couldn't contain himself. Today's grand opening of his business, Propane Bonanza, required everything from the pot-bellied businessman. For starters, the parking lot had a giant tent serving up free barbeque. Patrons were lined up around the block with paper plates ready to be filled with steaming hot meat. There was a moonwalk in the shape of a castle where kids jumped and hollered. Clowns mixed with the crowd making balloon animals for the kiddos. Another booth was frying up funnel cakes. Chuck had spent a mint on this event. He was as much excited as he was broke.

The sight of the police squad car pulling up to the scene made his stomach drop to his feet. *Shit in a sausage. They're going to ruin everything. Instead of painting a picture of a middle-class family trying to make it in a tough economy, people are going to think we're a bunch of assholes who belong in the back of a squad car.*

Did my son stick a firecracker up another poor animal's butt again? Is Angie peeing in public again? Last time she made lemonade under the blue sky, she was playing crash cars with her brother in one of those expensive grocery store shopping carts.

I'm going to have a heart attack.

So much money wasted.

Now I got a heap of bad publicity coming right my way.

Which one of my kids is in the back of the police car?

The officer didn't approach Chuck. He cranked up his bullhorn. Panic overtook the normal authority in his tone.

"Take shelter! It's headed this way. Listen. I can already hear it coming. Fireball is on his way. Run, before you get burned!"

Above Propane Bonanza, a hulking shadow touched down on the building's roof. Its body was bright as the sun with fire. Fiery plates and scales on its body glowed a neon red. He imagined if blood was fire, that would be the giant's color. Propane Bonanza imploded beneath its incredible weight.

My building!

You have no idea what I had to do to make this happen. I'll be making loan payments from beyond the grave.

Whatever you are, I'm going to kill you!

Enraged, Chuck ran to the semi-truck parked at the side of the building. They were delivering a fresh shipment of propane tanks and accessories. Chuck picked a tank up and hurled it towards the monster.

"Eat that, you flaming asshole!"

The propane tank burst from the extreme head exuding from Fireball's body. The explosion was the equivalent of someone flicking your ear really hard to the beast.

Fireball opened its gaping furnace for a mouth and unloaded a burner jet of flame that coated the entire parking lot. People were being cooked down to resemble what was covered in barbeque sauce on their plates. So hot, folks were melted into the pavement. Families wailed in terror, dodging the flames that danced everywhere.

Chuck could see the horrible climax to this terrible attack.

The semi-truck filled to the brim with propane tanks was showered in a downward plume of flames. A sonic boom explosion chewed up everything for a quarter of a mile. Chuck watched his life, his dreams and aspirations of being a businessman, go up into decimated ruin. A split second later, no traces of him would be found. He had been reduced to ash, along with everyone else at the grand opening of Propane Bonanza.

GOT A LIGHT?

"Got a light?"

"No. You're supposed to be quitting. You can't smoke without a lighter. If you can't smoke, I guess you'll have to quit."

Max Penderson was craving a cigarette. He made it this morning without one. He wouldn't make it much longer, being finals week. He walked with his friend, Johnny Comber, to their next class together on the Yale Campus. They were both majoring in engineering.

"Try vapor," Johnny suggested. "It's healthier. I love vaping. Give it a shot. It helped me quit cigarettes."

"Screw vapor," Max scoffed at his friend. "It's like a flavored asthma machine. Tar me. Nicotine me. Impurity me. I got a cigarette. I just need a light."

"You need to quit those cancer sticks. Vapor America! Join the revolution. Let's put the tobacco companies out of business. They're jerks. Ever since they got rid of Joe Camel, smoking's not any fun."

"I don't need a damn cartoon camel to tell me smoking is fun. I know smoking is fun. Anybody got a light? Anybody?"

Students going in each direction to their next class shook their heads. Everybody who used to smoke was now using vapor.

"Am I the only one in the whole campus who doesn't use vapor? Does anybody just happen to have a lighter because they like to flick their Bic for fun? For the love of Pete. My mouth's watering thinking about a smoke. A real smoke."

"I got apple pie flavor," Johnny said, offering his e-cigarette. "Give it a try."

"Apple pie flavor? Get that thing out of my face."

Sirens wailed on campus. Everybody stopped and looked around. The warnings sounded like the sirens that occur before a tornado was to touch down.

Max watched three of the main buildings be pulverized by a fast flying giant. Bricks and concrete showered the area, pounding people into the ground. Yale was ablaze with wildfire. Dorms were being smoked out of people. Throngs of terrified students were fleeing for their lives. Fireball took advantage of their vulnerability and rained hell on them. Cooking flesh scents filled the air. People danced and shrilled in terror as their bodies were blackened and eaten away. Many were instantly vaporized by the extreme heat.

Johnny was about to run in the opposite direction when Fireball touched down. Its foot squashed Johnny. Guts and blood shot out in both directions of the planted dragon's foot.

Max stood there peering up at the enormous beast. Being so close, Max's cigarette was lit. He didn't get to enjoy that precious toke. The dragon stomped him into the ground next for the hell of it before delivering fireballs that cooked the entire campus to a crisp.

FUN PALACE

The new Las Vegas theme park was built south of the big strip of casinos. Chris Manson was twenty-one, single, without a job, and ready to blow his parents' money on a weekend of Las Vegas fun. Today, he was enjoying Fun Palace, the largest theme park and fun resort in the city.

The operative word being *was* enjoying Fun Palace.

Now Fun Palace had been renamed Death Palace thanks to Fireball.

Treasure Island, Caesar's Palace, The Mirage, every hotel-casino had been leveled by Fireball's whiplash tail. Buildings were toppled and thrown into each other. Fireball uprooted buildings only to smash them down into the streets, squashing the crowds of horrified tourists into toothpaste. The destructive beast reached into buildings to collect a crowd of people into its hands only to squash them. Blood and limbs dripped out the cracks of its fists and pelted the war-torn streets. Walls of dust obscured the distance, punctuated by wild balls of orange death. Those pumping quarters into slot machines were crushed, cooked, and devastated.

B2 Bombers and other military jets were hovering in the sky, blasting missiles in Fireball's direction. Fireball spat streaming jets of fire and caused the incoming missiles and the jets themselves to erupt into heavy metal devastation.

Fireball spread out its wings and headed straight for the fun-time amusement park in the desert. The crowd saw the death dragon incoming and dispersed in terror.

The roller coaster, The Devastator, was spinning upside down when Fireball bashed its head against the track. The track warped. A line of carts flew off the track and landed right into Fireball's wide open mouth. It crunched on steel and human flesh with pleasure.

Tube City, a gigantic water slide, was assaulted next. The tubes were blanketed in piping hot coils of flames. The poor victims enjoying the slide were cooked so hard, when they plopped into the pool at the other end of the tube, their bodies sizzled when splashing into the cool water. The dragon disassembled the tubes and shook free anybody else inside into its hungry mouth and crunched on them.

Fireball kicked a moving Ferris wheel, causing it to roll into the desert at such high speeds that those riding it suffered broken spines and necks.

From across the park, the dragon was fueled by the sight of blood. It craved more death, more destruction, and it had so much more to give.

Flames from its two tiny holes for nostrils blasted forth, striking those playing mini golf so hard that it dismembered the victims before scorching them black. The golf green was now orange with burning flames.

Chris wasn't sure where to run. In front of him, a carousel kept spinning as it showcased people with their flesh melting like putty against the insane fires. The giant video arcade building was a toaster oven kicking out the reek of well-baked humans.

He had only one shot of escaping.

Chris snuck into the area with the go-carts. One go-cart still had its engine running. Someone had abandoned it on the track. He hopped in and started driving. He crossed through a grass hill and snuck between two other roller coasters that only had burning cars and no passengers. He dodged running persons and charred, roasting bodies strewn everywhere. If he could make it out of the park, maybe he could survive.

The problem, other persons decided to take the go-carts. He was driving side-by-side with frantic go-cart drivers. Chris dodged those who jumped and weaved into his imaginary lane.

He didn't have time to flip anybody off. Fireball was hovering over them. A talon came down and poked one driver through the skull and lifted the jittery and twitching woman into its mouth. It hand-selected two others, sticking them in their heads with its talon and throwing them into its mouth. Every go-cart driver suffered the same fate.

He was the last one remaining.

Chris knew his fate.

"You're not eating me!"

Without anywhere else to go, Chris floored the pedal. He drove into a steel pole. He was thrown from the go-cart. He planned on slamming headfirst into the pole and dying a quick death.

His plan failed.

Fireball snatched him in its mouth mid-air and swallowed him whole.

UNITED NATIONS

Secretary of State, Kim Stoner, was present on the behalf of the president and vice president of the United States. Not that her presence helped calm anyone at the United Nations headquarters. The room was a madhouse of arguing representatives from across the world. It was a happy accident that Fireball's attacks occurred during a normal meeting at the facility. Stoner raised her voice into the microphone to regain the auditorium's attention.

"We have to calm down. This is a time for reason, not panic. It's clear nobody is behind this incident. The following we now know with absolute certainty. Fireball appeared out of a dormant volcano in Hawaii. This monster can move itself from place to place in a blink of an eye. It vanishes, and then reappears hundreds of miles somewhere else to strike again. This creature is deadly as it is magnificent."

The roar of public officials from across the world overwhelmed her pitiful attempt at calming the mob. Officials were pushing, shoving, and a few, were even fist-fighting in the aisles. Stoner couldn't believe her eyes and ears. They were casting blame for what was currently happening on other people. Who could create a creature like Fireball? This wasn't a chemical or nuclear weapon. This was a living monster. An earth-born enemy.

Stoner had to do something extreme to regain the attention of the crowd. The future of the world was at stake. This wasn't a regional problem. This was a global crisis. They were facing the possible extinction of the human race.

Stoner removed a snub-nosed revolver from a hidden pocket of her red pantsuit. She shot a bullet into the ceiling.

"Now listen up, everybody! America can't take this threat on alone. We've hit that wall. Diplomacy is out the window. North Korea, I know you got nukes. Anybody else out there got nukes? Now's the time to use them. Every sanction we've put on weapons is temporarily put on hold. Unleash your biggest and best guns and blow Fireball back from wherever he came from!"

This got the United Nations' attention. The reaction to Stoner's command was mixed. Some were thrilled, while others were mortified.

The Russian representative was all smiles. Japan gave a bow and stepped out of the auditorium. France's rep was shaking his head in distaste. Brazil's person was making calls on his cell phone.

The time to observe her fellows had ended. A giant crash brought Stoner to the ground. It happened in two seconds. The roof of the building was gone. A tail had skimmed off most of the building. They were exposed, covered in the New York sunlight. The auditorium was under siege.

Fireball wasn't going to burn them alive. He balled-up his enormous red fists and started bashing those in the auditorium. Those fists owned such crushing power that those attacked were left splattered on the tiles. The lizard seemed to enjoy the sound of cracking bones and cries of terror abruptly reduced to silence.

Stoner stood at her podium and couldn't will herself to move. She knew all hope was lost. The exits were congested with fleeing representatives. They were quickly torched with flames. The reek of cooking flesh, the sound of high-pitched "I'm burning" screams stole away her will to live.

"Goodbye, humanity!"

She pressed the gun to her head and pulled the trigger.

CONSTRUCTION EQUIPMENT DERBY

America's Mega Mall was under construction in High Tower City, Michigan. Jimbo Thompson was work site supervisor. Everything was going great with the building of what would be the world's biggest mall in history ever.

Then out of thin air, the giant red dragon materialized. One moment, the top of the third floor in progress was unoccupied, then the next, the beast was smashing through it with its thick skull. Wings destroyed three levels, battering them into useless wreckage.

"Sir! Sir! You hear what they're saying on the radio! A monster is coming! It's destroying everything in its path."

"Open your eyes, Carl," Jimbo growled. "There it is. Big as ever. Forget the project. We got families to protect."

Police sirens wailed in the near distance. In another minute, cops would surround the place. Another minute was too long to let this ultimate beast have its way with the city. He had two kids, and another one on the way.

He would stop this beast in its tracks.

"We have to kill this thing! Who's with me?"

Jimbo stood alone. Each of his crew had fled the scene. That left the best man to face the monster one-on-one. He could see fires burn in the distance. Residential towns were ablaze. He could hear the swell of panic surround him. Screams of victims resonated on repeat. The highways were packed with people trying to evacuate the city.

By the time you would get home, you would either get killed, or your family would get killed. I'm not showing this monster my back. I'll show him my face.

Hit him with everything you got.

End this right here, right now.
You can't talk down a monster.

Jimbo raced across the work site and started up a crane. This was the one for the wrecking ball.

"Come here, you red asshole. You want to burn something? Try and burn me!"

The dragon monstrosity had its back turned. The wrecking ball was making good speed. The ball slammed the monster smack in the middle of the spine. Fireball unleashed a pained shriek and smashed into the six-story hospital. The hospital collapsed against the weight of the beast as if the structure were made of popsicle sticks.

A wall of dust obscured the area. Jimbo remained seated in the crane. The sound of chaos didn't end with the felling of the monster. Jets zoomed in the sky. Ambulance sirens echoed from every pocket of the city.

And red eyes glowed through the thick of the dust.

Those demon-cherry eyes were focused right on Jimbo.

This time, he was attacked by a dose of fear. He had seriously pissed off the monster. Jimbo scrambled with the controls. Another dose of wrecking ball would serve the creature right.

Fireball gave him plenty of time to swing the wrecking ball. He aimed it right for the monster. Then Jimbo was blinded by intense firelight. Out from its mouth, a giant ball of fire exploded. The blast bashed into the wrecking ball so hard, the wrecking ball came off the chain. The ball was hurled right on top of Jimbo, crushing him dead.

Fireball watched him burn for a moment before going back to the task of destruction.

GO NUCLEAR!

Ted Yearling was sweating and drinking at the same time. No amount of whiskey could calm his nerves. Fireball was laying waste not only to America, but also to foreign lands. Only adding fuel to his headache, his vice-president, Gary Botts, was being a real asshole.

"We're in a real shit pickle," Botts yelled, stomping about the presidential conference room. "Our troops have been crushed, and that monster hasn't even broken a nail. The shit's getting thick, and it's a stinkin'. If you don't shovel it up and bury it in someone else's backyard soon, we're going to have a real problem, Mr. President."

General Sharp was on the other side of the room thinking to himself. The other Joint Chiefs of Staff members were arguing back and forth about what to do next.

President Yearling poured himself another drink and didn't add to the conversation.

General Sharp was next to address the room. "This monster obviously has an instinct for war and self-preservation. It's destroyed munitions plants in Kansas. Fireball's already burned every nuclear and weapons facility worldwide. At least the nations with worthy firepower, that is. We're the last ones with nukes ready to be deployed. I say we do it. What say you, Mr. President?"

The president's words were slurred. "No other countries have nuclear weapons at the ready?"

"I'm afraid not, sir," Sharp informed. "France was even ready to contribute. The Frenchies always want to stay out of war. Now they want to start throwing punches. Fine. But Pierre will owe us one. So will everybody else, for that matter. We'll be the world's superpower. Think of our economy. Think about foreign relations. We'll be superheroes if we stop this monster right now. You can't have diplomacy without a bit of nuclear capabilities."

Botts tried his version of reaching the president. It was like talking to a little child, the vice president thought. "Think of it this way. New nuclear technologies. It's what hemorrhoids did for anal discomfort."

That made Ted laugh.

Any mention of anal things perked up the president.

"You think this is the right move?" the president asked Botts. "I mean, what if this doesn't work? What if we contaminate our own people? I could be like Hiroshima all over again."

"You're not Harry Truman," Gary said. "You are Ted Yearling. Our nuclear technology is world's better than everybody else's. We can limit the risk of harming innocents by targeting a specific area without high populations."

General Sharp jumped into the conversation. "Fireball's been spotted in Arizona. The Red Desert, to be exact. We can send a nuke his way and limit the risk of harming our own. He keeps jumping from place to place. The window is closing. Give me the green light."

The other Joint Chiefs of Staff agreed.

Nuke Fireball.

Ted Yearling took another sip from his highball glass and slopped some on the front of his suit. "Damn it. Okay. Nuke the thing. Just stop the killing."

General Sharp phoned in the order. "One nuke, sir, coming right up."

Fireball was scavenging the Red Desert for more towns to pummel and destroy when a sharp whistle disturbed it from its task. The sharp whine was getting louder and closer by the moment. Fireball rose up off of the ground and scavenged the distance in all directions to pinpoint the possibility of danger.

A heat-seeking nuclear missile was coming right for it. Instead of dodging it, Fireball's belly opened. The sideways gummy slit was a gaping opening. It swallowed the missile. Its belly closed up. A muted BOOM went off inside of the monster.

Fireball's eyes flickered from red to green intermittently. Thick black smoke exuded from its mouth and nostrils. The smoke was enough to obscure ten square miles in a gray soot cloud.

The monster started to have a seizure. Foam gathered at the sides of its lips. Every inch of it was covered in tremors. Its body was fighting to absorb the nuclear weapon. Fireball was about to topple over and slam into the ground when it was covered in green pulses of electric energy. It threw back its wings, unleashed a battle cry, and lightning bolts of green blasted from its body in all directions.

One green bolt traveled all the way to Asheville, North Carolina. It landed inside of a bat cave. Deep down, under millions of years of history, the rock walls seemed to open up. Awakened by the green bolt, out rose a giant Black Bat. It was easily the size of ten commercial airplanes. Black Bat bashed the cave to pieces to escape. Its body vanished mid-air and instantly reappeared next to Fireball.

Another bolt stuck hundreds of miles beyond California, deep in the Pacific Ocean. The bolt touched the ocean's floor, rocking the ground. The hole opened, releasing gouts of a black inky substance. Coming alive in that inky substance was a creature resembling a Manta Ray. Its body spun like a disc, rising up from the depths. The fifteen-ton creature towered over the ocean, spinning and hovering like an amphibious flying saucer. Like Black Bat, it was there one moment, and hovered in the air with its new friends in the desert the next.

Another bolt struck Texas. The hole it produced was so deep, fifteen city miles fell into the giant gaping hole. On the way up, an enormous prehistoric brown-plated Centipede crawled topside, cracking with green nuclear energy.

One more branch struck St. Pete Beach, Florida. Bashing up from the forgotten depths of the ocean, Crab battered its bulk to the surface, crawled on tops of buildings in search of why it was reborn after millions of years of slumber. Both Centipede and Crab vanished in a blink and reappeared in the desert.

All five creatures were there one moment, unified, and the next, they vanished. The monsters, owning jilted nuclear energy power, could go anywhere they wanted to destroy.

And that's what they did.
Destroy.

HELL ON EARTH

The Pacific Ocean was ablaze with aircraft carriers turned into blackened husks. Shrapnel from attack jets was spread out along the ocean top. Pilot Rick Ransom observed this from his B2 Bomber. The first line of defense against what was allegedly a "gigantic fire creature" had failed miserably. The threat had turned Hawaii into a death zone.

Ransom didn't believe it. He talked to his fellow pilots already in the air. They too agreed their superiors had made a great mistake. A blunder would be an understatement. The idea of their strategy being a mistake grew more and more ridiculous as they circled the area.

No monster anywhere.

Where is this deadly creature of fire?

This beast is nowhere to be found. Somebody's getting shit canned by the end of the day.

He circled around again and had to check his wits. An incoming ball of fire consumed the B2 Bombers in front of him. Spinning upside down full-tilt, Ransom had to shake the shock and steady his hand to fly and fight.

Once he got himself together, the B2 Bomber was right in the face of Fireball. The hot breath it expelled at the aircraft melted the steel, warping wings and cooking Ransom alive in a foul-smelling steam bath.

The pilotless B2 slammed into the water, erupting into fuel-ignited pieces.

Fireball watched the B2 Bomber crash. The monster sensed more threats beneath the water. The beast opened up the special glands between its plated body. Tar black grease covered it from top to bottom. Protected from the water, the monster dove headfirst into the ocean.

What it sensed were submarines. Fireball used its wings to displace water, delivering massive forces of motion. So intense, the motion battered the walls of the submarines so hard that the outer protective walls crunched and ripped. Crew inside were smashed by the cabin pressure. Fireball swam through the easily defeated collection of submarines, wading through severed body parts, guts, red-colored water, and quickly returned to the surface.

The black grease covering it had washed off. The fire instantly returned, burning hotter and brighter along its entire body.

Fireball closed its eyes and vanished into thin air. It teleported itself to Air Force bases across the country. Fireballs rendered collections of battle tanks, choppers, aircraft carriers, and even Army, Marine, and Naval training bases into smoking hot smithereens.

Threading through space and time, Fireball flickered out of sight and reappeared in North Korea, blasting secret nuclear bases and turning the areas into nuclear-infected horror zones. Russia was next. Fireballs covered the landscape, turning every military outpost and troop zone into burning cinder ash piles. Japan, Canada, France, the list went on. Nothing was left to survive. Missile silos, munitions plants, and military vehicles were not spared the wrath of fire. Fireball traveled across space and time and vaporized the world's armaments.

Radio and news reports spread the word of Fireball's deadly attacks. Fireball hadn't stopped with military bases. The Eifel Tower was knocked over by Fireball's wings, crushing hundreds of fleeing spectators. A CNN broadcast was going out when the reporter, John Whetley, was crushed by Fireball's red-plated foot at his anchor desk. Universal Studios was attacked while a group of filmmakers was filming *Dino Attack 3*. Fireball spat ten blazing balls on the studio, roasting the fake dinosaurs along with hundreds of crewmembers. Legendary Route 66 was literally a burning highway of exploded cars and people melted into the pavement as they fled for their lives.

Fireball's friends were also on the warpath.

Centipede tunneled into New York subways, latching onto moving subway cars. Hundreds of legs battered the outer shells, crunching the cars and those inside until the blood and guts of passengers burst from both ends.

Black Bat ended up in Pittsburg, screeching at the top of it lungs. The sonar pitch was so loud that it burst every person in the city limit's eardrums. Then the screech caused the victim's heads to burst against the punch of the pitch. Reporters refused to report the Pittsburg incident, because for one, nobody had survived, and two, the pictures that did come in, showed city miles full of headless bodies twitching and bleeding out. Black Bat was busy drinking the blood flowing from all directions in the streets.

Crab attacked the dock of St. Pete Beach, Florida. The giant crustacean used its mega-sized pincers to half commercial boats and dismember crews.

Suction was a spinning disc flying across the Midwest. Like a tornado, it sucked up people, cattle, and any animals into his manta ray belly-mouth and devoured them at hundreds of miles an hour.

Death tolls mounted fast. Thousands of kills turned into hundreds of thousands, and soon, the casualties reached the millions mark. News of the beast attacks spread globally.

Then, without reason, all the monsters vanished. People didn't know whether the monsters were gone for good or just taking a break. The Red Cross and emergency crews across the world did their best to save survivors of the attacks.

The devastation had occurred in only a matter of hours.

That's all it took to nearly destroy humanity.

The destruction was far from over.

The monsters would return.

Fireball's next target: Alaska.

THE ONLY HOPE

President Yearling didn't bother pouring himself a glass. He drank whiskey straight from the decanter. He saw the footage of new monsters being spat out from the earth. How Fireball simply swallowed up the nuke missile and turned that weapon into its strength.

"Unbelievable...just...so unbelievable..."

Vice President Botts was standing beside General Sharp. They had left the president on the other side of the room alone. "The president's a pile of worthless jelly. I say we do whatever we want. He can't pee in the toilet straight, never mind run this country."

General Sharp sneered. "Things are going to Hell in a hand basket. We only have one more option before our world is conquered by that thing."

Botts rubbed his exhausted eyes. "Another option? That's wonderful. I thought we were out of options."

General Sharp smiled. "You act as president, because jackass over there is pissing in his pants right now and is unfit to do anything for anybody. Give me the full authority for the next attack. No questions asked."

"And that would be allowing you to do what?" Botts asked, sensing apprehension from the general at the question. "Look, I'm not questioning you. Tell me the basic nature of your attack, and I'll sign on the dotted line. That's all I ask."

"I run projects that are indirectly funded by the government. Our taxpayers pay for new weapons research under the table. I have a group of people I can use to help us. This is experimental weapons of the future. Serious ass kicking power.

"Word is, our Fireball friend and his gang of uglies have been attacking Alaska like crazy. They've stayed there for several hours. They show no signs of moving on. There's something there they want. You let me fly out my people, and they can take them out while they're in one spot. Time is of the essence."

Botts didn't have to consider the request.

"Anybody who is willing to go into the danger zone and eliminate the target is allowed to do so, General. You have my full authority."

General Sharp shook the vice president's hand. "Thank you, sir. Your poise in the face of calamity is commendable."

General Sharp made his calls.

The Vice President just made the general one rich son-of-a-bitch. He had money tied up in investing in new weaponry of the future. Fireball would be the perfect testing ground for these experimental weapons. Once Fireball was wiped out of existence, money for new research and weaponry would come pouring in. Fear got the cash machine churning.

Yes, General Sharp was a very, very happy man.

The monsters had returned.

They were spotted in the most unlikely of places.

Troops were headed for Alaska. Aircraft were flying out these weapons. He prayed Fireball didn't leave the area.

Becoming filthy rich aside, this truly was the world's last chance of surviving true devastation. So much was riding on this battle.

He prayed for the future of humanity.

PART TWO: JOURNEY TO ALASKA

THE TESTICLE KICK HEARD AROUND THE WORLD
BEFORE THE ATTACK

Monica Lake had never kicked somebody so hard in the balls. Today, she broke the world's record.

Guinness would be calling her any day now to record the data.

How many pounds of force had her foot expended to crush those nuts? Her boss's pathetic mewling gave her a few hints. The pervert weasel was on the floor cupping his jewels. Drool trickled from his fat lips. The man's eyes were crossed. Monica hoped they stayed that way. She wanted the bastard to have to cup his balls until the end of time. He would go to the grave with his beanbag in his clutches. The open casket funeral would be hilarious.

Mr. Moody, the head of Polar Security Services, was starting to get himself composed. Ten minutes later, he was finally shaking it off. His normal penetrating sneer, the intimidating sizing you up expression, was bolstered to a new level of contempt. The man's bald head and lack of empathy for the human race really turned him into a maniacal Lex Luthor type.

She wanted to laugh at him. He should've sounded diabolical. His voice was a few octaves too high from the blow to the balls to sound tough.

"I could fire you for that. I don't care what you tell people what happened here. No one will believe you. You assaulted me. Do you know who I am? Does the Moody name mean anything to you? I get what I want because of that name. Moody means many things."

She wasn't having it.

She had met the man's type before. They thought because their father owned a big security company, and they were loaded with money, that they could do anything they wanted, because they were the boss, and you needed this job, so put up with my flirtations, or lose that said job.

She wasn't having it.

It was her first day on the job, and Mr. Moody gave her an assignment. She was to be a security officer for the grounds of a rental storage unit in downtown New Jersey. Once she was on her way out the door, Mr. Moody gave her ass a smack. That smack inspired her to turn around and kick him in the nards.

"I don't have to take your harassment," Monica said. "I might be on parole, and yeah, I do need this job, but I'm not putting up with sexual harassment. I'm filing a report."

"You go ahead and do that. Yes. Do that. We'll see how things turn out for you."

She made her dramatic exit out of the Polar Security main office feeling emboldened.

The next day, she would realize this was the worst thing that could happen to her.

Her life would soon come crashing down.

LEGAL COUNCIL

The next day, Monica hired a lawyer to take on her case. A Cliff Mullins became her lawyer. She visited his office, and Cliff, a middle-aged attorney, advised her on the situation.

She sat down in front of his desk. "Well, do I have a case? Certainly other women have experienced sexual harassment at Polar Security before."

"None of that matters, Ms. Lake. You see, there's a charge pending against you."

"Yeah, I kicked him in the nuts. Of course he'd file assault charges against me. The man is pure evil."

Her lawyer sighed. Sympathy weighed in his eyes.

"I'm afraid that's not the charge. Mr. Moody claims he found marijuana in your locker."

"What? That's bullshit!"

She burned with anger. She didn't have weed in her locker. She didn't smoke it, sell it, or own it. Where did this charge come from?

"You have to do something for me. It's not true. He's lying. You have to believe me."

"I'm afraid he's got proof."

"But it's a lie. He planted it in my locker. That's the only way. You're my lawyer. Do something on my behalf."

"I'm here to advise you. Mr. Moody has five signed and notarized letters saying you tried to sell them marijuana on work time."

"I know his play." Bitter tears were stinging her eyes. "He knows my previous record. He's taking advantage of me."

"That's just it, Ms. Lake. You've been out of jail for approximately two months. You had a drug possession charge with intent to sell on your record. You were paroled, and already, you're facing new charges. They'll give you hard time. I know the judge. He's lenient the first time. The second time, he throws the book at you."

That charge was also bullshit. My boyfriend stashed drugs in my car and was driving my car to make deals at night. I had no idea until the cops pulled me over for a broken taillight and searched my vehicle. He got off scot free, and I went to jail. He never visited me, or anything.

And now this is happening.

Nobody ever believed me.

They didn't believe me then. Why would they believe me now?

I had a scholarship. I was getting straight A's in college. I was on my way. My second chance has already expired. It's like the world wants me to fail.

"Mrs. Lake? Mrs. Lake? Hello. Are you listening?"

She was snapped out of her thoughts.

"Yes. Sorry. Please help me. I didn't have weed in my locker. Mr. Moody's covering for his sexual harassment. He's a bad man. He's done this to other women, I'm sure. We have to stop him."

"We could go to court with what you're saying, if that's what you want. But I guarantee you, you'll lose. You'll go back to jail. I'm talking hard time. Ten to fifteen years. Maybe more, Ms. Lake. Do you want to leave something to chance, or do you want to take the deal?"

"Huh? What deal?"

Mr. Mullins put his hand into hers. The touch of his hand made her jump. She was wound tight and ready to burst with a myriad of emotions.

"Look, Monica. Can I call you Monica? We could fight this. It'll cost thousands in attorney fees. The case will get held up in court for a year, if not longer. Mr. Moody is the type to pursue this to the fullest extent, and he's got the cash to do so.

"You're in a tough spot. I advise you to take the deal only because by the time you honor that deal, you'll be free again. Otherwise, you'll be chained to this case that you have a strong chance of losing. You're only twenty-two. I know you don't have much money. Not that it would matter. It doesn't matter if you're right or wrong. Mr. Moody's case is tough to beat. Right or wrong doesn't matter, I'm afraid. It's the unfortunate beast we call the legal system."

She could feel her world sinking.

Would her life become one screwed up situation after the other? At every turn, somebody else would be ready to take advantage of little innocent Monica Lake.

She barely mustered the energy to ask the question. "What's the deal?"

"You work for Polar Security for one year, and all charges would be dropped."

"I don't want to work anywhere near the bastard. I'll go crazy."

"There's one other thing."

"Yes."

"You'll be doing security work...*in Alaska*."

SMOLDERING ISLAND
DAY OF TERROR

Brian McCullough couldn't take one step without crunching on cinder ash...or the broken remains of another blackened skeleton. Waikiki was an island of ruin. Smoke continued to unfurl from lava holes and cracks in the earth. It was hard to imagine a city was once here, with a thriving tourist industry.

Brian McCullough was director of The Geological Survey. He was called out by the government to try and explain what happened here. He toured the island by helicopter, searching for answers. When he found the giant gaping hole in the middle of the island, he told the pilot to touch down and take the expedition on foot.

The gaping hole was as wide as six football fields. He didn't know how deep the hole channeled. There was no end to its depths. Smoke still rose from the magnificent drop.

He was talking to himself. "No weather patterns or warnings. The way the magma sprang up from random pockets of the earth, it makes me think something forced the lava up from the earth. This isn't naturally occurring. No doubt in my mind."

Brian paused. He found what looked like a big lizard's scale on the ground. It was bright crimson red and thick. It was the size of a shield. He rapped his knuckle against it. It tinked liked solid steel. He opened up an extra-large specimen bag and placed it inside. He would have to have his buddy back in Washington study it.

The government didn't need him on this job. This wasn't a naturally occurring event. This was something bigger than that.

Brian studied the lizard's scale in the bag.

This shocking find was new to him, and he had many friends in the paleontology and geology fields. He couldn't wait to show them his find. They would analyze the heck out of it. This find would earn him grants and oodles of funding. He would put geology and science back on the map. Finally, kids would want to grow up doing his job.

He continued his tour of the island.

The scientist found no survivors.

ALASKAN DEPARTURE
BEFORE THE ATTACK

Monica was half-way through her second screwdriver drink. She sat alone in the backmost seat of Alaskan Airlines. She couldn't steady her hands. She kept trembling on and off with anger and helplessness. She couldn't even focus on the *Sky Mall* catalogue. Those always made her laugh.

The events during the past few days kept recycling in her mind. Mr. Moody's deal expired in twenty-four hours. She either accepted the job in Fedora, Alaska, or she faced criminal charges. That meant serious jail time. She didn't have a choice. She had to accept the deal.

What else could she do? She was twenty-two, broke, and without a family to back her up in this trying circumstance. Most of her old friends didn't keep in touch with her. They didn't want to associate with an "ex-con." Considering most of her old pals were honor roll students, they considered Monica a drug trafficker. She was a hardened criminal to be avoided.

The end result remained the same. She accepted Mr. Moody's deal. The week flew by fast once she made that tough decision. She broke her apartment lease. She sold her car. The items she couldn't sell, she had to donate to the Salvation Army. That left her with whatever items she could fit into her carry on. Clothes, mostly, and a new set of thermal duds for the Alaskan climate.

Mr. Moody left a voicemail on her phone the day she signed the one-year contract to work for Polar Security.

"Hi there, Ms. Lake. Just wanted to inform you you'll be wanting a change of wardrobe. Where you're going, it gets mighty cold. You'll be shivering in your cute little shorts. No hard feelings, right? If you ask me and the authorities, I'm being rather lenient on you. I guess I can't resist a cute face. It's too bad things

didn't work out at our location. I won't be seeing you anymore. Well, make the best out of things. Build a snowman while you're down there. Hah. Hah."

Remembering the call, a sudden wave of anxiety swept over her. Monica got up out of her seat and rushed to the bathroom. She locked it behind her and splashed water into her face.

It's not fair.

It's not fucking fair.

Lies.

They're all lies, and I suffer the consequences. My life wasn't supposed to turn out like this. I wish this on nobody. Everybody thinks I'm a druggie. I'm not!

You have to calm down. You're going to lose it. They'll strap you down in your seat like those other people who lose their cool on planes.

Perspective.

Get a grip.

I'm Monica Lake. I'm twenty-two years old. I'm an ex-con. Nobody believes you're innocent of the charges. You've been dealt a shitty hand. The cards are covered in shit, and you have to stack them up anyway.

You were doing great. You had a scholarship for community college. You were getting your general education out of the way.

Then you dated Travis. You went on three dates with the punk. Then he wanted to borrow your car, and you let him, and boom, he stashed marijuana in your car, and I got pulled over, and I took the wrap. It's bullshit. Bullshit. BULLSHIT!

Voices of her parents spoke to her in her head. They were berating words. Scolding tones. Words weighed by heavy disappointment.

"Why can't you admit you were dealing drugs, Monica?"

"Once you turned eighteen, you're on your own."

"The law is the law, and you won't learn anything if you don't suffer the full consequences of your actions."

"You weren't raised to make dumb decisions like this."

"When you're out of jail, prove to us you can strive for success. But you're on your own this time. Don't come to us asking for money. You have to achieve on your own merits."

Her parents were happy to see her out of jail. They weren't unkind. The drug charges broke their hearts. Besides the hugs, and smiles, and well wishes, and I love yous, they didn't offer a home or a chance to get back on her feet.

She was on her own.

Just like now.

All alone.

She couldn't tell her folks about Mr. Moody's trumped-up drug charge filed against her. They wouldn't believe it. Pleading her case to them would only insult them.

You have to get through this.

This doesn't mean you can't get back on your feet. You can still go to school and do good. You'll show the world you can't take down Monica Lake.

People have been through worse and still turned things around.

Monica breathed. She didn't think anymore. She gazed into the mirror. She had a soft-featured face, though hard lines had formed around her eyes and mouth. Monica called it life's wear and tear. Her black hair was cropped below her ears. She had bright green eyes slightly bloodshot from the screwdriver drinks.

You deserve a good life.

You'll get it.

No man is going to ruin me.

Monica returned to her seat after drying her face off. She decided not have any more drinks. The rest of the flight, she slept. Soon, she would arrive in Alaska.

ALASKA ARRIVAL

Monica hailed a taxi once she picked up her luggage from the terminal. The cab driver asked her where she was headed. She gave the cab driver an address.

"Fedora? That's a bit out of the way. You have the cash? I'll take you if you can pay. Forgive me. I've been stiffed lately on the higher mileage fares."

She assured the surly driver she had the funds. She had no other means of transportation. The cab was the only option.

Once the cabbie started driving, she could tell the cabbie felt bad for giving her a hard time about payment.

"Let's start fresh. You new around here?"

"First time ever."

"How exciting? What brought you here?"

She could write the driver a book on how the world screwed Monica Lake. "A job. Let's leave it at that."

"There's not much out the way of Fedora. It's mostly a college town. Oh, there's also the research lab and the dig site."

"Dig site?"

"Yeah. It turns out because of this global warming thing, certain sections of the permafrost have forked and cracked. I read it in the newspaper. I guess they've been able to drill and dig, and luck would have it, they've found some dino bones and other things. It's kind of hush hush. The crew out there have been at it for a few months. The site is in the university's backyard, practically. Are you a student?"

She told him no.

Monica wasn't in a great mood to talk. The cab driver had no problem keeping the conversation going by himself.

"You got the dig site about fifty miles out from town. In town, you got a residential community. A few hundred people live out there. We'll blow by it soon. We're in the city right now. Lots of people here. Out in college town and the dig site, it's a barren ice cube. At night, it gets crazy dark and crazy cold. Cold enough to kill you.

"You're obviously from the mainland. A space heater won't cut it out in this cold. Don't push your luck. Hypothermia is a very real thing."

Monica tuned out, and then randomly tuned back in.

"...as far as wildlife goes, you got black bear and caribou roaming about at certain times of the year. I had a buddy who was attacked by a bear once. He lost his right leg, but he lived. My buddy, he hunted that bear down. He has that beast's head on his wall. Talk about your revenge. You take my leg, I take your head. I say the bear got screwed on that deal."

"Yep."

She wanted out of this cab in a hurry.

They passed by the bigger city, with its wild sprawl of residential and commercial spaces. They bypassed civilization and were on a two-lane highway. She was stuck with chatty for another forty-five minutes before Alaska University appeared. The building had dormitories that were five stories high. Around the area were restaurants and other apartments.

Across from the university was the building for Polar Security. Mr. Moody's father owned almost three hundred businesses in the United States. This was the farthest one from Mr. Moody himself. She was grateful for that one favor.

The building was small and made of brick. A painting of a giant polar bear was the building's logo.

This was her destination.

She paid her fare and the cab returned in the direction of the airport. Monica stood there in the freezing cold. The winds were harsh and biting. She could only imagine how cold it would be at night. Shivering in place, she decided to get on with it. There was nothing left for her to do but enter the building and meet her new boss.

WELCOME TO POLAR SECURITY

"You may notice you're in Alaska. Yeah, it's cold here. Guess what? The citizens of Alaska know that. They've known that since the beginning of time. We're a bunch of ice cubes in an ice cube tray. It's as cold as a witch's tit on her dying day. It's as cold as free-on. It's frigid out there in that Alaskan permafrost. We get it. It's chilly outside. Do us a favor and don't mention it. Most people on our staff have lived here their entire lives. They're familiar with the weather patterns. We're over it. There's no use complaining."

Monica sat there in front of Chip Dugan's desk listening to him talk. Her new boss was a burly son-of-a-gun dressed in a black thermal coat with the Polar Security logo on the right breast pocket. That image was of a Polar Bear standing on top of an igloo, looking regal and proud. Chip's beard was thick around his face and tri-colored. A mix of brown, black, and lots of gray. He was over three hundred pounds and full of dry humor.

He smiled at her. "You think I'm joking? You don't think I'm serious? Go ahead. I'm giving you the chance to get it out of your system."

"That's okay. I won't mention the weather."

"You're a bit soft spoken, newbie. You're from New Jersey. I was expecting a bit more attitude. I promise you can say anything you want about the weather right this moment. You can even use bad words."

"No. I'm good."

"Now you sound like a mouse. I'm going to have to buy a super-sonic hearing aid to hear you talk. I'm not trying to make you even more soft-spoken by teasing you. If you're going to work here, I want you to have fun. Be yourself. None of this 'sir this,' 'sir that,' 'reporting for duty, sir.' Now in Mr. Moody's report, he said—"

"It's colder than an Eskimo's cooter! There. Happy?"

Chip busted up. He leaned over his desk, smashing his gut against the wood. "Hah-hah-hah-hah-*haaaah!* Cooter? I haven't heard anybody use that word in forever. Wonderful. I knew there was a fire in you. Sometimes the pilot light goes out, I guess. Fantastic. You're hilarious. I love it."

Monica's face showed anything but good humor. The mention of Mr. Moody hardened her face. She couldn't hold back her animosity for that creep who took advantage of his money and position to mess up her life.

Chip sensed her mood change. He was immediately apologetic.

"Hey, I get it. Yes, I read the report. I don't care what it said. I believe in fresh starts and new beginnings. I also got to read your statement in response to Mr. Moody's allegations. I know you're a good kid. Anybody who reached the highest merit in Girl's Scouts has to have something going for them. Yes, I know that about you. Plus, you had a 4.0 in college. Amazing. I can't even read a page out of a book without getting distracted.

"It sounds like you had a few roadblocks in your life. Let me tell you, I won't be one of them. You come to work on time, do your job, and don't call in sick like crazy, and we'll get along famously. And yes, it's colder than an Eskimo's cooter."

She couldn't help but smile in relief.

"There. That's better. We're not jerks here. We're a busy place. Polar Security has many accounts. A few patrol the power plant down the way, just to keep out trespassers. There's a mall back in Fedora where many of our best keep a lookout for shoplifters. I got a couple out at the university who do rounds. You can't be too careful these days with all the school shootings these days. Sad fact.

"I have a shift opening. I think you'll love it. It's not easy. It'll be strictly night shift. Have you heard about the dig site out behind Alaska University? Pretty wild. The permafrost shifted, or broke, or whatever, and a crew from the university are excavating what could be a piece of history. Cavemen is what I hear. Nothing's been confirmed.

"Anyway, I want you doing night patrol on the dig. They're deep under the ground. They've built scaffolding to get down there. All you have to do is patrol the levels, make sure nobody's trying to do damage to the excavation sight, and we're good. If you're ready, I'll start you tonight."

"Yes. I'm ready to work."

"Great. I'll pair you with Bob Berger. He's a good guy. One of our most seasoned security officers. The best thing, the university is in walking distance of our headquarters, right here. I understand you just got in town, literally. Do you have a place to stay?"

Oh no. He's going to ask me to stay with him...if I treat him nicely.

Chip read into her facial expression. "Man, Mr. Moody must've done a number on you. When you're the son of the boss who owns the company, it's like you automatically become an asshole against your will. I'm not like that, Ms. Lake. There's an apartment building two blocks from the street. It's four hundred dollars a month."

She heard the number and couldn't believe it. "Four hundred dollars a month? You know I'm interested. That's great."

"That's the spirit. Now contain yourself. Here's Deb's business card. This is totally legit."

She accepted the pink business card. She turned it over and saw a drawing of a lady hanging upside down from a stripper pole in lingerie. The card read: *Deb's Debutantes Club.*

"Is this a joke?"

"It's funny, but no. Not a joke. A few of your co-workers stay there. You see, the club is on the bottommost level of a three-story building. Those other levels are rooms for tenants. Deb takes care of everybody...upstairs and down. I used to live there before I got married. It's clean, respectable, safe, and best of all, cheap. I always had a bed to sleep on and heat in my room. Life don't get much better than that."

Chip was reading her vexed face.

"Think it over. I can show you other things. The rest of the lodging is further out. There are the dormitories. Of course, you have to be a student to live there. Anyway, think it over."

He handed her a sealed box. "This has your work coat, a few uniform shirts, and the employee handbook. Meet Bob Berger here at ten o'clock sharp. He'll show the ropes, help you get your feet wet, and we'll be on our way. I'll have a schedule made for you by then. I'll post it on the hallway way out there. If you have any questions or issues, please, always feel free to talk to me. My door is always open."

He shook her hand. "Glad to have you here, Monica. I look forward to getting to know you better."

She shook his hand with a sigh of relief.

Chip Dugan was nothing like Mr. Moody.

It still didn't change things.

She was stuck here for a year.

CONCERNING FACTS
DAY OF ATTACK

Brian McCullough had visited the scorched birthplace of Fireball. Now the director of The Geological Survey was grounded at a small military base in Honolulu. The helicopter that delivered him to the island earlier had no choice but to land. Everywhere across the world, devastating attacks continued.

After leaving the chopper, he was met with a fellow field researcher who also worked on and off for the military. Her name was Lt. Sarah Glendale. She studied a mix of marine and biological threats. She was very much a professional and to the point. After walking through armed military figures, Brian was ushered underground into the actual military base. He was taken specifically to the lab.

He soon learned the real reason for their abrupt landing.

Lt. Glendale wanted his sample from Fireball's body.

She studied Fireball's scale under a microscope. "We're talking millions of years old here. At least. Our friend here had a long nap in the lava, and he's full of fire."

Brian gulped hard. "This plating…it looks impenetrable."

"Tests will provide that information. The naked eye can't determine that. Thank you for providing the sample. We're lucky to have it."

"You should've seen the island," Brian said. He wanted to unload what he witnessed. The bones of corpses. The hundreds of bodies not quite completely charred poised in agonized death poses. "It's all gone. Fireball torched the place. Those poor people were burned alive."

"That will be all, McCullough."

"I'm sorry. What?"

"The sample is all I need from you. Tests will be done immediately. *You* have a different set of concerns altogether."

"What do you mean? I feel you're so many steps ahead of me."

A stern-faced man entered the room with a flat-top haircut. He was a hard-bodied sergeant by the name of Chambers. He was in his middle age with enough hard lines to prove he had seen many harsh and bloody battles. He tongued a wet cigar in his mouth and gave Brian a once-over. Disapproval computed in his stare.

"This is the guy they're sending with me on assignment? I bet he's never fired a gun. He probably can't even pee straight. This wimp is supposed to help me accomplish my mission?"

The lieutenant didn't want to be bothered with complaints. "I'm not the one who assigned you this guy. Chances are, everybody else available is either tied up trying to stop those monsters, or McCullough is it. We've suffered staggering casualties."

"I'm not holding his hand," Sergeant Chambers complained. "Eggheads are worthless on the field of battle. Instead of talking with a machine gun, he wants to talk with a pen and a pad of paper. Well, fuck that."

Brian was about to voice his disdain when the sergeant was handed a walkie. He answered the call.

"Yes, General Sharp. Of course. The president has given the order. I'll make the calls. It's good to hear we're finally launching some serious firepower at this thing."

Sergeant Chambers grabbed Brian's arm. "You're coming with me. Alaska, here we come. Future monster grave sight. I'll throw Fireball down into the hole, and you'll cover the grave."

"I don't understand," Brian said. "Where are you taking me, and why?"

"Fireball has stayed in Alaska. Intelligence claims he's after something there. Here's our chance to put him down. We want you there with us to document the process and to pick up the pieces of the creature and put them in neat little bags so you can study them. That's why you're coming with us, Mr. Geological Survey. Whatever the fuck that is, anyway. Buck up, pal. It's time to blow this threat off the map."

Brian boarded the military aircraft begrudgingly. Question marks and concerns flooded his mind. One thing did make sense. What the sergeant said was correct.

He was on his way to Alaska.

DEB'S DEBUTANTE'S
BEFORE THE ATTACK

Monica was hit by a powerful gust of wind on the way out the door of Polar Security's headquarters. Light snow was falling from the sky. The area was already covered in three feet of white from a previous front. She read the forecast all week. It was going to drop below freezing, and they would be hit hard with snow. The soft fluffy stuff falling from the sky didn't keep her from venturing across the street and over a block to the building Chip recommended. The apartment building stood out among its neighbors. There was a postal office, a hardware store, bar, drug store, and further down, a general store.

Deb's Debutante's was a three-story building among these businesses painted an ugly shade of pink. The sign for the strip club was right above a stairway leading to the basement level. Beside those steps was another set of stairs that lead up to the actual lodging.

She wasn't sure where to go to find Deb herself. Monica made her way down the stairs to the club. When she opened the door, she was greeted by a muscle-bound bouncer type in a tight top named Bo.

Bo spoke in a thick voice. "You here for a stripping job, or are you here for a place to rent?"

"A place to rent, please."

She blushed at the thought of the man thinking she was going for the stripper job.

Bo yelled across the room. "Hey, Deb. You got a tenant here."

Monica couldn't see inside. She was still standing outside. A voice yelled back, one sounding older and gruff. "Yeah. You know her?"

Bo looked her up and down. "Nope. Sure don't."

She spoke timidly. "Chip Dugan recommended me. I'm working for him as of today."

"Chip Dugan?" The crotchety woman's voice carried from across the room. "Why didn't the lady say so? Bring her on in. Chip's word is as good as God's. I love that man."

Bo invited her inside.

The strip club wasn't anything fancy. There was a bar on one side. Then there was the stripper stage. It had a runway with four poles. Surrounding the stage were tables for the patrons to enjoy the show. Mood lighting was suspended from the ceiling. Right now, the lighting was normal. She could see the blues, reds, and green lights overhead for the after-hours entertainment.

A woman spoke from another room. "Offer the lady a drink, would you?"

The bouncer guy pointed at the bar. "You want a drink, ma'am?"

"A Diet Coke would be great."

"On the rocks. Coming up. Diet Coke."

"It looks like she's got you doing everything here."

"That's my mother. We're a good team."

"Oh."

She almost burst out laughing. A mother-son strip club. The idea was amusing.

Bo's eyes widened. "Oh wait. No, no, no. It's not like that. She's *like* a mother. We're not actually family. She took me in like a son. That's all. Tough story. I was going out for Mr. Olympia. You know, the muscle guy competition. I was training hard before the next competition. I did something bad to my back. Really jacked it up. I gained weight, I was depressed, because I couldn't compete anymore. Deb gives me a job. The moral of the story, I swear we're not banging. But if you look at her old pictures, she used to be quite the debutante. Those tits could defend America. She could swing 'em to make you cry. Here's your Diet Coke."

She accepted the glass.

Deb called her from another room. "Come on in, honey. I'm ready to see you. Let's have a visit."

That voice, Monica thought, she kept imagining a female version of a greasy club owner. Monica was tested again not to laugh. The woman had to be in her late sixties. She had dyed blonde hair put back in a bun, huge '80's green shower curtain earrings, and the brightest pink lipstick she had seen painted on lips in years. The shirt she wore was a cartoon drawing of breasts where her actual breasts would be.

Bo was right. She had a crazy rack. She could swing 'em to make you cry.

"Pleased to meet you, Mrs...?"

"I'm single. My name's Monica Lake. I literally just flew into town."

Deb eyed the luggage she was carting around on wheels.

"Oh, bless your heart, dear. You're beautiful, you know that? I'll say this once, and I'll leave it on the table. If that security job don't work out, you march on down here and you got a job. No offense. You're beautiful. You'd melt the polar icecaps, sweetie.

"Anyway, that's the business woman in me talking. Never mind me. I speak freely. When you've been alive as long as I have, you lose your filter. Or I still have my filter, it's just very dirty."

She stuck out her tongue and bit it playfully.

"Um, I was here about a room."

"Yes, of course, sweets. Do me a favor and take it all in first."

Deb was talking about the pictures hanging up on the walls behind her desk. They were pictures of a younger, leaner, sexier version of Deb's former self. She was dancing burlesque on a stage for U.S. soldiers during the Vietnam War. Another showed her swinging a hula skirt as a background extra in a Frankie Avalon beach party movie. Another showed her in a slasher movie. She was running from a machete-wielding killer in the film *Party at Sheckler's*.

There were photo stills from other bit parts in movies. Others were headshots to promote her modeling career.

"I danced, I stripped, I acted, and now, I'm a business woman. I had a good run. I was a real hot tomato. Once you get so old, you can't cover it with make-up anymore. Once you can't bounce that quarter off your rump without it getting caught under a flap of skin, your career is done. They call it the quarter test. Swear to God it's a real thing.

"I enjoyed it while it lasted. I'm not ashamed of it either. All women should be proud of their sexuality. I'm glad I didn't live in the Victorian Period. They would've had me shot.

"Know this about living here. I have shows in the evenings, and longer shows Friday and Saturday nights. If your moral sensibilities are tested, like the folks down the road at the church, then this is not the place for you. The walls in this building are sound proof. You won't know we're even here. The sound of titties shakin' won't stir you from your sweet dreams.

"The only riff raff are the occasional drunks who try to take it out of their pants when they should be keeping it in their pants. This isn't a flop house. You also got the boisterous, douchebag college students who come here to blow off some steam. They get loud and stupid sometimes. Sheriff Kolke handles them. Always call 911 if you feel like something serious is going down. So after hearing all of that, are you still interested in living here?"

"What's the rent?"

"Four hundred. If you're a friend of Chip Dugan's, I don't ask for a security deposit. The deal is, the cash is up front. You got the money, you got a room. Easy as that."

Deb lit a cigarette. She blew a smoke ring with her paw out for the cash.

Monica dug it out of her purse. She had six hundred cash. That left her a little wiggle room before pay day.

When the money landed in Deb's palm, the woman gave a small shudder. "I love the sound of cash crinkling in my hand. My ears are fine-tuned to that special sound."

Deb had her sign several pages of forms.

"Sign here. Sign there. And here's your keys. And your card."

Monica put the keys in her pocket. The card was a plastic pink card that read Deb's VIP Patron Card.

"Hold onto that. The card means your first drink per visit is free. It's a thank you for staying with us. We're very glad to have you. Your room is on the top floor. That's room 302. If there's any questions, my phone number is on the back of that VIP card. It's a direct line. Bo can fix most anything. He's a renaissance man. And a handsome slice of beefcake, if you ask me. Doesn't hurt when they're easy on the eyes."

Deb gave her a wink.
Monica shook her hand and headed up to her room.

WELCOME HOME

The apartment wasn't anything special, nor was it something terrible. She had a working shower. One bedroom. The kitchen was too small. The living room was just big enough for a couch and a stand with an old school box television set. They had Wi-Fi Internet. The heater was a big metal unit in the corner that hissed and coughed. She expected Bo to visit many times to fix the archaic thing.

She showered, changed clothes, and opened the box Chip gave her back at the station. There was the Polar Security thermal coat with hood and gloves. She anticipated the cold and already had boots, long underwear, and long johns.

The airplane trip left her exhausted. She slept for five hours. When she woke up, it was nine o'clock p.m. That left an hour before she was to meet Bob Berger and start her evening shift.

Deb had a welcome basket of food on the kitchen table for new tenants. She ate an apple, heated up a cup of noodles, and ate two of the candy bars. She had a pot of coffee brewing before the end of the junk meal.

She sat alone, blowing the steam off the top of her coffee mug with the *Deb's Debutante's* logo on the side. Monica thought about her situation. The forced move to Alaska. The sexual harassment. The trumped-up drug charge. How her family loved her but still had those ill thoughts lingering in the back of their minds. *Our daughter is a drug dealer. Our sweet girl takes drugs. Our girl has ruined her future by making bad choices. We love you, kiddo, but you're on your own now.*

She couldn't help but cry and feel sorry for herself.

Her spirit felt as cold as the thick permafrost that Professor Randall Sterling was excavating right this moment.

THE DIG

Half a mile from Monica's new apartment was Alaska University. The university was mostly empty at this late hour. Some students were attending night classes. The night howled with gusts of an incoming weather front. The next days promised heavy snows. How bad was yet to be determined. The local meteorologist was anticipating three to six feet of snow.

The weather didn't matter to the head paleontologist and tenured professor named Randall Sterling. The seasoned professor had every reason to be motivated and love his job. He wasn't grading papers by students who didn't care about the subject he was teaching.

He was closing in on a big find.

Some would say the find of a century.

A year ago, he was a teacher who wouldn't have any profound effect on science. His name wouldn't land in any scholarly papers. He wouldn't get crazy funding for the science department to pursue scientific matters.

It all started when the earth shifted a quarter mile south of the university. Global warning, some blamed. The land behind the university was a fifty-mile stretch of permafrost. That permafrost had cracked, imploded, and revealed a big gap deep under the ground.

That gap was a time capsule in history.

First, they discovered tools cavemen used. Wooden spears. Pelts. Tools dating all the way back to the Paleolithic Period.

Yeah, big deal, Randall thought. It was crap tourists purchased at a museum's gift shop. Funding didn't come from trinkets of the past. The paleontologist community wanted bones, bodies, and better yet, well-preserved remains from things that once lived millions of years ago.

The better find was the perfectly preserved Glyptodon. He likened it to a giant armored armadillo with a huge bludgeon for a tail and a hulking protective bone shell. A photographer from *Paleontology Monthly* visited the campus and took Randall's picture beside the hulking two-ton creature.

The professor had theories about the special fifty-mile stretch of permafrost. The earth had shifted 2.5 million years ago and had rearranged landmasses across the globe. This shift had dumped a variety of creatures and life forms across continents into one place.

Right here in Fedora, Alaska, he believed.

He couldn't prove the theory. He was trying to further theories already advanced by paleontologists and geologists in academia previously. Randall questioned himself on a regular basis.

Am I furthering theories on their merit, or do I want these theories to be true on the basis of how fun it would be to find these relocated life forms?

He imagined cavemen sharing the same icy grave as dinosaurs.

Randall had the quotes from the article repeating in his head every day, motivating him to find everything that could be recovered from the dig site.

"*Professor Sterling and his colleagues, alongside his son and wife and selected students, work tirelessly to undercover history millions and millions of years old.*"

"*…dig site had the potential to be the best spot for specimens in decades.*"

"*…paleontologists from around the world are flocking to this mega site to pitch in and help.*"

"*When it comes to cutting edge science being used in the name of paleontology, look no further than the dig site at Alaska University.*"

After finding the Glyptodon, funding came from everywhere. Machines and technology were flown in to puncture through the permafrost. Powerful machines that would've cost millions of dollars to rent. They had channeled thousands of feet into the earth. Scaffolding had been built so the crew could either walk or use the elevator installed on site.

The problem was, after the money had been spent, nothing else had been found.

Not a damn thing.

Interest waned on the dig of the century. The professionals from across the world had left the project in frustration. Reporters and magazines left Randall hanging out to dry. Now his name would be associated with failure.

He had a month left of funding.

Randall stayed motivated, because two weeks ago, they finally found something very promising.

They were currently thawing out a scene cut right out of time. A family of cavemen. Randall and his crew were chiseling them out and fighting the inclement weather to free them. They were perfectly preserved.

There was something else they would find.

Randall had no idea it was there.

They would accidentally bring back to life America's only hope in defeating Fireball.

FIRST DAY

The afternoon's snowfall had amounted to two feet. Trucks had already cleared the roads and salted streets and sidewalks. The night was deep set in darkness. Streetlights illuminated the way. Monica walked the two blocks to reach Polar Security headquarters. She entered the building to find Chip was about to sign off for the day. Another manager was working in the office. She didn't come out to greet her.

Chip apologized. "You'll meet Angela sooner or later. She's really busy at the moment. You're very much needed, Monica. They want more security guards at the dig site. Randall Sterling is onto something big, and he wants to protect his investment.

"I think the guy's a bit desperate. I'm all about finding cool stuff in the ground. This place was hopping with media and reporters and sciencey people. Then the dig site turned out nothing. But the way it sounds, he's hit pay dirt. You should be excited. You're headed right there soon."

He directed her to the schedule and then said Bob Berger would be there any moment to show her to the job. Chip said goodnight and left the building.

She waited alone in the building's break room. She filled a thermos with coffee and indulged in a day-old chocolate donut with sprinkles.

"Filling up, huh?"

Monica didn't hear Bob Berger enter the room. He was barely five foot tall. Bob had the likeness of a fat elf with a big bald head and goofy grin. Bob Berger was in his forties. He had a gut that spilled over his belt. Despite the grin, his eyes said, 'I'm always tired, and I don't have time for your problems.'

"What do you mean by that?"

Bob stood in front of the vending machine. He inserted a ten dollar bill. He pressed a dozen different buttons. He stuffed bags of chips, candy bars, and other snacks into the various pockets of his thermal pants and coat.

"You got to fill up. What else do you do when you're walking in circles all night? I eat. It's perfect, because by the end of my shift, I get a sugar crash, and I sleep hard. I love it."

He retrieved two cokes out of the vending machine.

"You ready for patrol?"

Monica held up her thermos of coffee. "Sure am."

"You need more than that. Ladies choice. How about something from the vending machine? Something to gnaw on during the long night of the dark soul?"

"What are you talking about?"

"It's boring out there. You got an iPhone? The rule is, if you keep one ear bud in, and keep one ear open, you can listen to music or podcasts. I love podcasts. I'm usually listening to the ones talking about wrestling. I love wrestling. Any kind."

"I'll be okay."

"How long have you been a security guard?"

"It was after my first day I got a transfer. So I guess this is my first day of actual work."

"You got a transfer on your first day? Huh. Interesting. You must've ruffled the wrong feathers."

Bob sensed the change in her demeanor.

"Oh sorry. Too personal. You just met me. You seem nice. Shit happens. I'm sorry."

"Shit does happen," Monica agreed. "Bad shit."

He shook her hand. "It's great to have you on board, Monica. Consider yourself lucky. I can teach you the tricks of the trade. I've been doing this shit for fifteen years. I don't know why you let Chip talk you into doing dig duty."

"Dig duty?"

"The dig site. It's bo-ring. Most of the people working are too caught up in what they're doing to talk to you. That's key. Find people to talk to. You have to shoot the shit with folks. Talk to people even when you don't like them. It burns time. I have a PhD in fucking off. It's an art form. I'm the master. I'll teach you."

They walked together up the street to the university. It was almost ten o'clock by the time they bypassed the university parking lot and the building itself. Behind the university, everything seemed to end. There was only an endless horizon of solid white with a reflective glaze of ice.

Monica had to open and close her eyes repeatedly.

Was this for real?

There was a literal square cut out of the permafrost. The square was the size of her apartment building. There was no telling how deep the hole channeled. A roof was built over the hole to keep out the snow. Plastic walls sealed in the sight. The plastic flapped in the hard gusting winds. The winds were so loud that they shut up motor-mouth Bob Berger. He was pumping her full of useless information about the art of fucking off when he realized he was yelling to be heard.

The areas around the permafrost seemed questionable. Chunks of the ground had broken or sank into the earth for miles in every direction.

When Bob parted the thick plastic curtains to enter the dig site, they could talk again. There was an elevator, which was a wooden platform on a mechanical pulley system, that was big enough to fit heavy-duty equipment. The square was surrounded by wooden scaffolding. She looked down the edge onto the entry of the scaffolding. The drop was endless. She could sense people at work down there. She barely caught the industrial lights shift and move below. She couldn't see the bottom of the hole.

Bob invited her to walk down the scaffolding with him. Every step, she could hear the crinkle of a different snack foods package.

"I'll admit, things have been much more interesting the past week and a half. You'll see what I'm talking about. They found some frozen cave dudes. Highfalutin Randall Sterling thought he was the bee's knees in the scientific community when he found that giant prehistoric armadillo thing.

"They had crazy machines tearing up the land. They had dynamite charges. Blew the shit out of stuff for awhile. I watched chunks of the earth just blow up. It's the most action this town has had in years.

"Funny thing is, Randall, getting his pretentious ego on, thought he was on top of the world. Then he doesn't find jack shit. Everything calms down. Rumor was circulating they were going to shut down the dig site. But maybe not. I wouldn't care either way. This place is boring.

"This is the job, Monica. You walk up the scaffolding. You make sure no bozos who aren't supposed to be here aren't making trouble. You go down the scaffolding and check for bozos. Rinse and repeat for twelve hours. You see what I mean? Bo-ring."

Bob's walkie went off.

"Bob, report in."

Bob rolled his eyes. "It's Angie. Chip is awesome. Angie's a fucking bitch. Anyway, you answer on the first call when Angie calls you up. If you don't, she chews you out. She'll think you got your thumb up your butt or you're sleeping on the job.

"This is Bob."

"We need you to report back to base. Ted called in. His ulcer is acting up again. We need you on Lock Up."

"I'll be right over, Angie."

He sighed. "Looks like you're on your own tonight. Remember. If you see any signs of trouble, don't intervene. You call the cops and stay away from the perpetrator. We're not paid for confrontation. If you need anything, I'm on frequency three. I'll be happy to answer any questions."

"What's Lock Up?"

"Imagine a giant car lot full of those giant storage containers. We don't know what's in them. We patrol the grounds and make sure nobody hops the gates and tries to break into them   Anyway, I have to get going. We'll catch up, Monica. Sorry I have to bail on you."

"That's okay."

She was secretly grateful. Bob Berger was a nice guy, but he was a Chatty Cathy doll. You didn't have to pull his string and get him to talk.

PhD in fucking off.

Give me a break.

It's like saying you're seasoned in diddling yourself.

That made her laugh. She was glad Bob wasn't around to see it. He would think she was crazy.

You're feeling like your old self again. You used to make jokes. You didn't used to be everybody's victim.

Thinking about what had happened to her sobered her up.

She had a job to do.

She was going to do it.

Monica marched down the scaffolding. Curiosity welled up inside her. She wondered what this dig site was all about.

She would soon find out.

VERBAL ALTERCATION

Every step down the scaffolding, a loud creek echoed. Monica wondered how sound the structure was under her feet. Every new level she walked downwards, there was a light installed on the walls housed in a plastic box. They shed a bluish hue up against the dark. Thick black power cables were connected to the edges of the scaffolding, snaking down to the bottom.

Bob was right.

Serious money had been put into this project.

She could still hear the wind flap the plastic walls from the top level. The way got colder with every tier of the scaffolding she descended. The thermal gloves, coat, boots, and long underwear failed to keep the chill from creeping into her bones.

Monica stopped to feel the walls.

They were solid.

Frozen to the core.

The longer she walked, the more she wondered how deep was this hole? Colder and colder the area became, and she was just starting to see where the scaffolding ended. The bottom level was encrusted in thick ice. Tunnels had been cut into that ice, channeling deep into dirt walls. More blue-tinted lights housed in plastic boxes lit the way. She heard what sounded like machines humming along with the tink-tink-tink of picks, chisels, and hammers clawing at ice.

She was too curious not to see what was going on. She walked through icy tunnel after icy tunnel. She almost slipped twice on the slick and uneven floor. Every breath she expelled, she could see it on the air. How many degrees below zero was it down here?

The tunnel continued. It was the darkest here. She could only see an orange speck far up ahead. The tunnel opened up into a wide room with many more dark outlets to journey. The wide-open room had a dozen people dressed in thermal gear working. Stage lights were positioned to brightly light the scene.

"Careful there! You can't puncture the specimens. You could damage what nature worked millions of years to preserve. Greatness up against clumsiness. Which do you prefer? You all will have a credit in this magnificent find if you do a good job. A's for everybody across the board, and the strongest recommendations for any job in the field you chose. So don't screw this up!"

"You hear that asshole talking?"

Monica was startled. She turned to see a younger man with rosy cheeks and an athletic build standing beside her.

"*Oh*. You scared me."

"Sorry. This place is pretty scary, huh? It's like a frozen crypt. I'm Ryan Pritchard. I'm one of the undergrads working on the project. I hope to get a full-ride scholarship out of my work here. We're Professor Sterling's drones. We've been chiseling out this room and aiming space heaters at dead cavemen trapped in hunks of ice for quite awhile. Yes, you heard me right. We're melting ice off dead dudes. If you look closely, we've almost freed them from their icy prisons."

She was fascinated by the dig site. The work. The magnitude of the find. Monica wanted to read more on the subject. She was studying the six tall human shaped hunks of ice scattered about the room. Professor Sterling, the guy wandering between persons chiseling and working at the ice, was pompous and self-involved. He had his long white hair styled in a ponytail and deep-set eyes that knew obsession very well. He was a man who had something to prove and was desperate to shove his superiority down people's throats.

"…you got any weed on you, or uppers, or anything to keep us going? These late hours are killer. Energy drinks and coffee aren't doing it anymore."

"Huh?"

"You're the new security girl, right? Monica, yes?"

"I'm Monica. I don't know what you're getting at, though. I don't deal drugs."

"I overheard that prick Sterling and his son back at his office talking about how the new security girl got a transfer here for dealing drugs. The professor said he'd watch you closely to make sure you weren't trouble. Me and my friends were hoping you could hook us up. We've been busting our backs extra hard for the professor. We were planning on mellowing out later. I could use a good high."

There was no build up to what happened next.

She couldn't contain herself.

She lost her cool and erupted.

"You're making an assumption. You assume what I was accused of really happened. You don't know me. I don't do drugs. I don't sell drugs. I'm a good person. I don't deserve this stigma you people put on me. You think I'm a dumb party girl who smokes, drinks, and sleeps with anybody. You know nothing about me, college boy. Nothing at all. I have nothing for you. I should punch your face in, you douchebag weasel. Don't you ever look at me in judgment ever again. You're probably here because mommy and daddy paid for it. They probably cut you checks for beer money. You screw around, you don't have to work all that hard, and you'll still earn your degree. I bet you'll probably end up making more than a hundred grand a year. You were probably born a frat boy. Anything you wanted, you got it, and you never had to thank anybody for it. I can't stand to look at you. Stay away from me with your requests."

"What's happening here?" Professor Sterling grabbed Monica's arm like a child's. "What do you think you're doing, young lady? You're interrupting a very important project. We're at the peak of our work, and you're here distracting my help. I talked to what's his face. Charles, no, Chip. I talked to Chip about you security guards sticking your noses into our business. I know what we do here is interesting. I'm only asking you to be professional and leave us be."

"But he came up to me, and asked me—"

"I don't care what happened. All I see is the new girl flirting and distracting my crew. I told Chip his new girl better not disturb my students. These students work hard and for no pay. We're achieving something great here. Go back to your patrol, and do your job. How dare you disturb us. That's why the last person got fired. You want to be fired too? I can arrange it. I'll snap my fingers, and you're done."

She couldn't believe what Professor Sterling said to her.

He had unleashed a string of verbal abuse.

She had done nothing wrong. Her processes were running full blast. Her nerves were uncoiled. She couldn't think anymore. She stomped away from the sight back towards the scaffolding.

"Dad, what are you saying? I saw the whole thing. She didn't do anything wrong."

"Son, get back to work."

Monica couldn't see who she could safely assume to be Professor Sterling's son through the haze of her teary eyes. The kid had hurried up to his father from a row of other workers.

She didn't care. She had to escape the scene. She burned with humiliation.

Everywhere she went, she was condemned to be unfairly treated.

The world doesn't owe you anything, she kept thinking. *You have to find your way. Somehow.*

Monica focused on putting one foot in front of the other.

Do the job, she thought. *Get through the night. You can break down   later.*
Up the scaffolding.

Down the scaffolding.

She patrolled around the entrance of the dig site. The cold winters only grew more bitter as gale force winds slammed into her body. The horizon was desolate and bleak with nothing but black distance and the increasing chill. The kind of chill that bored through skin and settled deep into bone. The kind of cold that caused joints to ache and bodies to tire.

She thought about turning onto channel three and asking Bob Berger for advice, or at least tell someone her side of the argument.

Would it matter?

Who would believe the "druggie" girl over an "esteemed" professor?

She had to laugh. Would they ship her off to another less desirable location in the company? They could fire her. Termination would be great. She could move on with her life. The year contract wouldn't matter. But would that bring back Mr. Moody's lawsuit? She didn't know. Maybe he would press charges if she got fired. That would mean jail time.

I don't care. Let them come after me. I won't back down next time. I'll talk over Professor Pretentious Windbag. I'll stick up for myself. I can take a pee test. I've never done drugs in my life.

She felt a little better as the hours ticked by. Her anger simmered down into a quiet boil.

Once it was nine a.m., she reported back to the Polar Security office. She met a few new co-workers during the shift change. The one that stood out was named Ted Higginbotham. He was a six foot tall, wide-shouldered, squared-jawed tough guy. He was pure intimidation with his bushy orange red beard and mane of grayish orange hair styled into a rat-tail. When he talked, though, he sounded like the nicest, sweetest man.

Ted offered her a seat in the break room. "I owe you a thank you. You covered my ass on your first day. My ulcer was acting up. My wife says I need to drink less coffee so late at night. But everybody knows me. I love my coffee."

Ted was the kind of person who could read a person easily, and that's what he did. "I can tell you're upset. You have a hard night?"

"I was doing my patrol, and one of the students asks me for drugs. I guess they heard about the reasons for my transfer. I'm sure everybody knows. Gossip gets around fast. I chewed the kid out for asking me, and that Professor Sterling guy gets mad at me for sticking up for myself."

Ted was genuine. "Look. Everybody judges everyone. I won't lie. People talk about why you were sent here. The student body at Alaska University shouldn't know about it. I'm sorry that happened, especially on your first day. My dealings with Professor Sterling have proven he's either the science dork you'd love to take classes from, or he's a hot-headed idiot. I guess you met the sour end of the deal."

She felt like she had to defend herself. "Listen. I don't sell drugs. I don't do drugs. That's all I can say, right? It's all he said, she said crap. Mr. Moody lied about what happened because he sexually harassed me, and I wouldn't take it."

He held up his hands. "Whoa. I'm not accusing you of anything. I get to know people and make decisions myself. I like to use the brain God gave me. I'm not a religious crackpot or anything. I tell this to everyone I meet who's been through hard times. People die every day. They didn't have the choice to do something about their lives because they're six feet in the ground. You have two arms, two legs, and your head is still screwed onto your body. A lot of people can't say that.

"If that positive sappy crap doesn't help you, I'm inviting several co-workers to my house this weekend. We'll get to know you. We'll dispel the rumors. You can come to the house, drink some beers, and shoot some guns. Drinking and shooting guns always makes me feel better about everything. You should come. I got the guns, the bullets, and beer."

Monica rubbed the fatigue from her eyes. "Absolutely. It sounds like fun. Thank you."

"Great. I have to get going. Work calls. Talk to you later, Monica. Hang in there."

She got a copy of this week's work schedule and walked home to her apartment. Students were heading to early morning classes. Trucks were making patrols laying down ice melt on the roads.

Deb was watching her worker, Bo, shovel the sidewalk in front of the apartment building. Monica said hello. Deb whispered to her, "Isn't he a nice slice of beefcake? Those buns. Oh, those buns. *Mmmm mmmm*."

She was too tired to engage Deb in conversation.

Monica took the elevator to the third floor. She undressed, showered, and collapsed in bed. She was working another twelve-hour shift at nine p.m. tonight.

She woke at five p.m.

Around five-thirty, Chip called her.

"I hope I didn't wake you."

"No. I'm awake. What's going on?"

"I need you to come into work about fifteen minutes early. I want to talk about what happened last night at Professor Sterling's."

She swallowed hard. "Sure thing."

"See you then."

Chip hung up.

Monica couldn't tell if this was going to be a good talk or a bad talk by the tone of his voice.

Great. Something to look forward to.

She was in walking distance of the local grocery store. She picked up some general supplies and returned home to unpack them.

Monica made herself a spaghetti and garlic bread dinner. She finished it, dreading the moment she would have to meet with Chip and talk about last night.

After making better coffee than what Polar Security offered, she gathered herself up and trudged over to the office. The dark cloud of concern loomed over her. Trouble was coming right her way. She entered Polar Security knowing she would have to defend herself once again from her detractors.

Chip was behind his desk in his office.

Professor Sterling was sitting in the chair opposite him.

They both turned their heads up at her.

Oh great. Now I'm in for it.

She entered the office, preparing herself for the worst.

HUH?

Professor Sterling got up out of his seat to shake her hand. "It's nice to see you again, Monica. I owe you a great big apology. I wasn't very nice to you last night. My son, Ryan, overheard the whole skirmish. You didn't do anything wrong. I blew up at you and said things that weren't correct. I'm either overtired, or I've had too much coffee. I'm sorry for the way I reacted." The professor gave Chip a glance.

The man was handing the conversational baton back to Chip.

Her boss struggled to speak.

He seemed embarrassed.

"I have to just come out and say it. I messed up. I talk to the professor about any of the new hires who may perform security on the scientific work site. Background and all. I told him about your situation back in New Jersey, and I told him details I had no right to divulge. Word got around to some of the professor's undergraduates and colleagues. I can apologize all day long and still not do you justice."

Professor Sterling gave her an encouraging smile. "This is the good part, coming up. Go ahead and tell her. I can't wait to see her face. She won't know how to handle this."

Oh great.

Here it comes.

Another piece of lovely news.

Chip was happier to speak now that he had made his confession. "The good part. Yes. It turns out the co-CEO of Polar Security has been doing unethical and illegal things for quite some time. Mr. Moody is in some hot water. He's his father's son, and when daddy owns the company, certain things get swept up under the carpet. Finally some dust escaped.

"Last week, a group of twelve ex-employees of Polar Security, all female, have sued Ron Moody for sexual harassment and blackmail. The cops questioned him, and Ron Moody cracked. He confessed everything. Including your situation."

Monica was literally sitting on the edge of her seat. "What are you saying? Please don't mess with me. This has got to be a joke."

Chip could sense she was about to pop. "Deep breaths, Monica. This is all good for you. I'm so very happy to clear things up. I've only known you a short period of time, and I already know you're a good kid.

"Ron Moody took advantage of your situation. He blackmailed you into signing a bullshit contract to work out here for a year. I guess Ron has a strange sense of humor. He likes to mess with people's lives. He's one of those, what do you call them?"

"Megalomaniacs," the professor supplied.

"Yeah. One of those mega-whatevers. Crazy guy, that Moody. This means a few things for you. The contract is null and void. The pending lawsuit has already taken care of that. Polar Security has hired a new CEO, and they're cleaning house. The Moody family is out. They're both on their way to jail. It's all pending, of course.

"Let me put this the best way I can. You're young, Monica. I have a feeling that prior drug charge when you were in college having to do with your ex-boyfriend is also suspect. You've had a bad run of luck. That's all in the past. Now you've landed on a pile of shamrocks."

"Get to the even better part," the professor insisted. "I want to see her face when she hears this."

Chip shuffled the pile of papers in front of him. "Well, Polar Security's legal team is working overtime to get things straightened out with Ron Moody. They're offering you a sizeable cash settlement. And a full-ride scholarship to a university of your choice. They haven't finalized the paperwork yet, but there will be a lawyer to talk with you about everything very soon."

Professor Sterling broke in excitedly.

"I want you to attend Alaska University. I like the way you stuck up for yourself last night. You don't take crap. I also know about your time in community college. You had the grades. I also know you're interested in the sciences. You should dive right in. Don't hold back. This is opportunity knocking at your door. *Hell*, it's trying to break down your door. *Hell*, you'll fall into a career if things pan out the way I think they will. Work for my team. I have several students graduating this summer. There'll be openings on my crew. I need good people like you. How about it? Please say yes."

"Think about it," Chip offered. "Look over the paperwork. Let it sink in. This is incredible. I'm just so very happy for you, Monica. I hope you stay on with us for the summer, until you figure out what you want to do with your life. Gosh, so much has happened, and it's only your second day."

They all laughed over that.

"I'm speechless," Monica said. "I'm about to burst into happy tears."

"*How about bursting into work?*"

The three of them turned towards the doorway.

There stood Angela. She only knew it was Angela because of the name embroidered above the breast pocket. Angela was in her sixties. She had curly gray hair, thick red glasses, and a deep-set stern expression.

"I'm not paying everybody to have warm, happy, glowing moments. That is excluding our illustrious professor. I've also been informed until the legalities are complete, we are not to make comments on Mr. Moody or Polar Security as a corporation. You've done your job, Chip. Monica here is informed about her rights. We'll have somebody from human resources take our newbie through the rest of it. Thank you."

Nobody moved.

"I said thank you."

Angela turned and exited the room.

Chip gave her the bird.

Professor Sterling stood up. "Can I escort Monica to the work site? I have something to show her before she gets to work. It's not against company policy to give people a lift, is it?" Chip groaned and rolled his eyes. "Hey, she's my boss. If Angie were a piece of gum, I would've spit her out a long time ago. She's not so bad once you get to know her. She's had it rough in life. Not all of us have hope for humanity. Yeah, give her a lift. I don't care."

Monica accepted the ride.

There was something very special happening below ground.

DEFROSTING HISTORY

Professor Sterling was throwing out his best pitches during the short ride to the work site. He parked in back of the university in a special dig site reserved space.

"I know most kids don't think 'Alaska' when furthering their education. It's a fine institution. We're known for our science. And right now, we're red hot. I won't lie. The dig hasn't gone so well up to now, but we hit pay dirt about two hours ago. I haven't slept in almost seventeen hours. We've broken free our cavemen down below. We also discovered more things. These will win us new grants and so much more. I wouldn't be surprised if they made a documentary about this place. I'm so excited!

"I've been trying to further previously stated theories. About two million years ago, there was earth activity that caused many land masses to shift and crash together. It's hard to explain, but imagine land masses tilting at an angle for hundreds of thousands of miles. All kinds of life forms were dumped here. The conditions were just right in this area that things have been perfectly preserved. The question that will win me many grants and serious attention is…what kind of life forms are actually here?

"I'm trembling talking to you about it. I need good students, and quick. I have nothing against hard-working people, but the second a slot opens, you should give those kind folks at Polar Security a two-week notice and sign on. Forget the notice. I can get you a full ride scholarship."

"Why offer me so much? You're being very nice. Don't get me wrong."

Her words didn't betray her emotions. Monica was on Cloud 9. She could barely feel her feet touch the ground. Everything in her life had turned around all over again. It was like the law of averages had exploded, giving her tons of good luck when all she'd had the past few years was shit dumped on her head.

"Because you're different. You're smart. The kids I got down there are smart. And they know it. They need somebody with a good solid head on their shoulders and real world experience to even them out. Plus, they're millennial children. Another word for selfish entitled brats. All they care about is partying, what's blowing up on their cell phones, and when lunch break and naptime is. I swear I'm a nanny to those kids. I wipe noses and butts when I should be uncovering the earth's deepest paleontological secrets."

Monica checked her watch. She had twenty minutes before getting to work.

"Don't worry about the time," Randall said. "I talked to Chip beforehand. He said I can show you this on company time. You see, this is what I mean."

"I'm not following you."

"Chip basically exonerated you of all charges. The company is going to pay out what seems to be shaping up as a handsome lawsuit. The company threw in a scholarship to boot. And you're still ready to work hard tonight. This is the kind of mentality most kids are missing these days."

She was touched by his words. "Thank you, Professor."

The professor let her ride the elevator down to the bottommost level. He was getting more and more excited with the ticking down of each level.

"You'll be one of the first non-crew members to see them. We'll have the media out here soon once we dig deeper into the site. There's so much we have yet to uncover. We're on the precipice of many good things."

They walked through the carved-out tunnels to the place where the professor had wrongfully chewed her out barely twenty-four hours ago. The same crew from last night were working tirelessly, using pick axes and finer steel tools to dig deeper into the room.

A row of space heaters were aimed at the caveman specimens in the center of the room. She had a better look at the walls. This was as if they were inside of a cave. There was a pile of sticks with a circle of stones around it for a fire. A spit made of broken sticks had a creature that looked like a cross between a house cat and a rat posed over what would've been a roaring fire.

The specimens captivated her.

They were very similar to the caricatures of cavemen in cartoons. They had the exaggerated brow. Their bodies were covered in thick coarse hair. The cavemen were much taller than she expected them to be. Some of them were almost seven feet tall. The four males were thick bodied and so powerful looking. The females weren't the prettiest, and that was being kind. They were smaller, slender versions of their male counterparts, with crazy hair, thick muscles, and dumb facial expressions to match. The group of them wore thick animal pelts and animal skins. The skins looked to be taken from bears. One of the specimens was a young boy. He had a permanent snarl etched on his face, like he was about to enjoy a juicy dinner right when he got flash frozen.

"Seven cavemen in total so far. There may be more. They're all intact. We can study them and answer a lot of questions about their survival and living habits."

The professor moved to a table covered in hi-tech gadgets. She showed him to a laptop computer. The monitor showed a blank screen with orange body heat signals. Those were the working crew. Beyond where they chiseled and hacked away at rock and earth, there were dozens and dozens of blue smudges.

"This is a thermal scan. It helps us know when we're digging pointlessly into the earth, or when we're onto something. It's called a KODOD Scan. Anyway, it's brand new technology. Those blue smudges you're seeing represent other life forms we have yet to uncover. Things are getting real good real fast."

"All that technology," Monica laughed, "and you're using space heaters to thaw our friends out."

"Yes. You use what you got. I want all the ice off of them. They still got some on their limbs. Their pelts will take the longest to thaw out."

"Okay, kiddo," the professor said, shaking her hand. "I hope you take serious thought about what I said. You should sign on with us in the fall. Sleep on it. You've had a wild turn of events, and I can't be any happier for you, Monica, no matter what you end up deciding."

Before she started her rounds of the property, the professor called back to her. "Monica, wait. I want you meet my son, Jeff. Jeff, meet Monica."

Jeff was the younger and better version of his father. He had handsome hazel eyes and a welcoming disposition. He had long blonde hair hanging loosely down to his shoulders. She shook his strong hand.

"I wanted to personally apologize for Ryan Pritchard's behavior. He had no right to ask you for drugs the other night. We suspended him from the dig for two days. Right when things are getting good. I say that'll show him."

"Thank you, Jeff."

"Can we talk later? I want to tell you more about the program."

His father gave Jeff a sideways turn of the head. Then he gave Jeff a "go get 'em" smile.

"I'd like that very much."

Father and son returned to their work. Monica started her shift. The night shift blew right by, having so many good things to think about.

DRINKS AT DEB'S?

Monica did her patrols. When she walked down the scaffolding, she could hear Professor Sterling going into command overdrive. He was talking up the dig, pretending to be writers from scientific journals who tossed up wild accolades, in order to motivate his crew. The professor was a grown-up kid when it came to paleontology.

It finally was morning time, and she signed off the clock back at the station. She ran into Ted Higginbotham there. He was signing on for the day.

"Monica, I heard the good news. Congratulations. Just so you know, me and a few of the other workers meet at Deb's Debutantes for drinks every Thursday. And guess what? Today's Thursday."

"Deb's? But that's a strip club."

Ted shrugged. "Hey, my wife comes along too. Besides, you live in the apartments above it, right? You can get tanked and not worry about driving home. The Thursday night drink specials are out of this world. Cheap is the good word.

"It's actually fun on Thursdays. It's Bingo night. You win prizes. Deb's real forward thinking when it comes to the strip club. College students love it. It's hilarious. Think about it. Besides, the strippers don't go nude until after Bingo. You won't burn your eyes. Otherwise, if it weren't for the gimmick," he cleared his throat and winked at her, "I wouldn't be caught dead in a place like that. We meet there at about eight o'clock. Eight-thirty is when the bingo gets going. Will I see you there?"

She wasn't sure what to say.

"Don't answer. Think about it. We'll only be a few flight of stairs away if you come and decide it's not your thing.

Congratulations again on the lawsuit. Sexual harassment stinks. Anyway, don't forget. Titties and Bingo at eight."

She couldn't help but laugh at Ted. The guy was such a goofball. Maybe she would go. She couldn't decide. She was too exhausted to give it much more thought.

She returned to the apartment and went right to sleep.

After waking up, Monica mustered up the courage to call her parents. She decided to doctor up the story of the recent events. She told them she was getting a scholarship, and was thinking about Alaska University. She described the cavemen Professor Sterling had shown her.

Both her parents were very excited for her. She hadn't heard them this happy in years about their daughter's life. Monica admitted to herself this was quite the proud moment for herself.

She showered, cleaned around the apartment, and decided maybe she would take up Ted's offer. Bingo and cheap drinks. Ted was also right. If things got too weird for her, she could just walk back up to her apartment. She wondered who else from Polar Security would be there. She assumed Angela wouldn't be there. The old bag was a total bitch. *"How about bursting into work?"* Who talked like that?

The decision was made.

She was going to drink, have fun, and be social. After all, she had a right to celebrate.

Her wardrobe was limited. She would have to hit the outlet mall in town. First, she had to get a car. Another first, she had to make friends who could give her rides and hang out.

She put on a pair of jeans and a long-sleeved pink cardigan. It wasn't anything fancy. Warm and appropriate for strip club Bingo. Monica had no idea how the world would change in the coming hours.

Soon, the terror would begin.

TITTIES AND BINGO

Ted and Chip were smoking a cigarette above the stairs leading into *Deb's Debutantes*.

"She's here!" Ted shook her hand. "I was worried. The look you gave me this morning when I talked about hanging out at a strip club. I thought I was either going to get slapped or high-fived."

Chip understood her position. "Most people don't go to the strip club with their co-workers to blow off steam. Keep in mind, this is the cheapest drink in town. I always have fun here. Deb's a riot. She's a local mainstay. You support the mainstays. I like mom-and-pop businesses. There's not much else to do in this town besides piss on snow anyway."

"You're forgetting one pastime. Shoot guns and drink," Ted offered. "We'll do that next time. I got the guns. And I got the booze."

"Ted loves his guns," Chip said. "He's got enough weapons, if the end of the world came about, he'd turn into Rambo."

"Minus the muscles and unintelligible speech." Ted stubbed out his cigarette. "Come on in, Monica. Let's play some Bingo and get to know you. Socialize with us. We're the security guardians of the universe. The super guards."

She walked down the one level of stairs down to the strip club. Bo, the bouncer, was dressed in a heavy coat and glittery earmuffs. Monica figured Deb put him up to that fashion choice.

"You guys ready for some Bingo? Deb's got some fantastic prizes for the winners. And for the new girl in town, you get two free drink tokens. Go wild. It's Bingo night!"

"Two tokens?" Chip gave Ted a funny face. "I only got one when I was the new guy in town."

Bo shook his head. "Just get in there. It's dollar drink night. You can't afford that, you need to go to the liquor store and drink at home."

"But my house doesn't have all this ambiance," Chip laughed. "This is my home away from home."

"Yeah, yeah," Bo said, brushing him off. "Just don't trip over yourself when the girls start popping their tops. Swear to God, I had these two idiots who came in here one time. They were sitting at a table, and his friend had tied his shoelaces together. Once the nightlife started, and the girls stripped on stage, he rushed that stage. The guy tripped over his feet and fell right on his face. Broke three teeth and his wrist."

"Why his wrist?" Monica asked.

"Because he had his arm extended with dollar bills on the way down. The idiot didn't bother to catch his fall. Keep your head on straight is the moral of the story. Now get in there and have fun. We love you guys."

The inside was lit a soft blue. The stripper stage was dark. There were two long tables set up in front of the darkened stage. Bingo cards were set in various places. Monica saw Bob Berger sitting on one end around five other empty spots. Counting Chip, Ted, Bob, and herself, who else did that leave, she wondered.

Deb, wearing a red-sequined skirt and a T-shirt that was a cartoon of a woman's torso in a bikini, whistled sharply at the group and then spoke into a cordless pink microphone.

"Games start in five minutes. Plop your butts down. I got some fancy prizes to give out tonight. We got an hour before our sweet honeys hit the stage. Your necks will crick when you gaze upon Cinnamon's tasty curves. You should see the hot rack on Bambi. You thought Mt. Everest killed a lot of men when they tried to climb its peaks? Try Bambi. She'll leave you dead in the woods like Bambi from that cartoon." Moans from the crowd followed that comment. "What? Too soon? *Bambi* came out how many years ago? Oh, don't worry. My jokes get worse.

"Now everybody, I have a question. Guess where our new girl, Roberta, has a flame tattoo on her voluptuous anatomy? Stay after Bingo and find out. We're open until one a.m. I'm Deb, your hostess tonight. Beers are a dollar. You people love thirsty

Thursdays. Shots are two dollars. Let's heat up Alaska. We're here to melt your hearts and your ice caps."

They met Bob at the table. He was half-way through a mug of beer. He was pulling out a small bag of chips from the side pocket of his khakis pants and munching. He said hello through a mouthful.

Monica joined Ted and Chip at the table. The tables were full of other patrons. There were two spots remaining at the table.

"Who else is showing up, Bob?" Chip asked.

"It's a surprise," Bob said. "You'll be shocked. I didn't believe it myself. Our guest said she wanted to celebrate Monica's big victory."

Monica was curious herself. "Then who is that other spot for?"

"It's for me," Jeff Sterling said, joining them. "I wanted to help celebrate Monica's big day. First round's on me. On behalf of the dig site."

"That's what, four dollars you're spending, big boy?" Chip joshed. "Thanks, partner. I hear you guys have something to celebrate too."

"Our cavemen, for one," Jeff explained. "And there's more we're still excavating. Something prehistoric. Serious history is going on right now."

Their other guest joined them. It was Angela from headquarters. She was dressed in her work uniform. "Hello, everybody. It's part of my job to act like I give a damn about you people. What is it? Bonding, or is it team building? I call it bullshit. If I act like I'm on the same level as you people, you'll do better work, or some nonsense. Yeah, whatever. I'm here. And congratulations, Monica. Two days in, and you've already shaken up the company. Great."

Deb returned, speaking into her microphone. Two strippers dressed in skimpy lingerie wheeled out a big cage full of Bingo balls. "Okay, lovelies. Spin them balls, and spin them real good."

Other sets of strippers in various bodices, lacey frilly numbers, and lingerie were acting as waitresses as they delivered drinks to the tables.

Their beers were delivered when Deb finished her opening joke, "...the dentist got fired because he was putting *his* root in *her* canal! Talk about your fillings! You better call the dental concession! Boy, oh boy! Don't forget to floss, right?

"Okay. Moving on. After everybody's recovering from laughing so hard, gather your cards. I'm going to start drawing numbers."

Everybody had their cards and the chips to cover their letters. Deb was yucking up the crowd. She was a female Mickey Rooney. Between announcing letters, she'd tell jokes about her saggy breasts and references to tube socks and loose change.

Monica couldn't believe it. She had a Bingo! She yelled it out. She went from excited to nervous when Deb came over to her, strutting her wide hips to make a huge show of it. She was reliving her better days in the skin business.

"Darling, what's your name?"

"Monica."

"Monica. What a pretty name, isn't it? I know you're new in town. You live here in this building, and I'm so very happy to have you here with us. She's single and unencucumber'ed. Wait, wait! I mean unencumbered! Boy, oh boy! Semantics.

"Sweet Monica, I'm going to ask you a very serious question. Have you ever had a penis whistle before?"

Monica's cheeks were neon red and pulsing hot. "No. I can't say that I have."

She could see her co-workers were busting up laughing, including Jeff.

"Do you know how to use a penis whistle?"

"No."

Deb pulled the whistle out of her pocket. It was a pink whistle in the shape of a penis. "Here you go, dear. You put the whistle up to your lips and you blow. Stuff will come out of it in no time."

The crowd was a drink and a half into the game.

They were starting to laugh at her terrible jokes.

Deb wasn't finished. "You ever bite a whistle, Monica?"

"No."

"Good! That's good. The men in the room can uncross their legs now. One less biter in the world. If you ever bite a whistle, it never works the same again, does it? Now when you give it a blow, all the men will come knocking on your door. It's a magical penis whistle. Use it wisely. Everybody clap for Monica! What a good sport! She's a lot of fun, isn't she?"

Jeff raised his mug to her. "Deb's great."

Everybody agreed about Deb's greatness.

"You people really come here all the time?" Monica asked those at the table. "I never worked for anybody who hung out at strip clubs."

"This is Alaska, honey," Angela said. "You have to do things you wouldn't normally do to get hot."

"Deb's the real pull," Ted explained. "If she were like forty years younger, I'd be all over that shit."

Bob was opening another bag of chips from his other pocket. "Deb could gum you real good. Take out her falsies and give you the thrill ride of your life."

"Just blow the penis whistle," Chip chuckled. "Your dreams shall come true. Keep your whistle in tune to the key of cock."

Deb kept calling out numbers.

Hot ladies kept delivering drinks. Monica's nervousness was melting away after the second beer. She didn't drink that often. Soon, she'd be swimming drunk.

Deb handed out other prizes. One lucky guy got a box of pasta in the shape of penises. Another lucky winner received a dildo you could strap to your head. The last winner won a ten-pound tub of strawberry-flavored body butter.

Deb had to say something about the body butter prize.

"The worst thing about these economy-sized tubs of body butter is that no matter what you do, pubes always end up in the butter. There's nothing you can do about it. You can check and recheck, and it makes no difference. You'll still get pubes. It's like a bar of soap. I always find pubes there too. Anyway, folks, the real show is about to begin. Don't you go anywhere. The night is only beginning. My lovely ladies are about ready to entertain you. Stay out of the snow and stick around."

Angela ordered a round of shots for everybody.

When the shots arrived, Angela held hers up.

"Shots on me. I'm feeling light in the head. That means it's confession time. I know I'm a fucking bitch of a boss. I've been married four times. I have three boys. They're all grown-up idiots. I act like something's up my ass all the time, and I apologize. I deal with four ex-husbands. I have too many stupid men in my life. On second thought, the problem isn't that I have something up my ass. No. No. No. I'm single. I haven't been laid in eons. The real problem is I don't have anything up my ass!"

"*Wh-aaaaaat?*" Chip was laughing so hard he had tears going down his face. "We'll get something up your ass, boss. It's my sole mission in life. I'll start petitioning the neighborhood."

"Here, here," Ted said. "To getting something up Angela's ass."

Monica was giggling. She couldn't get the words out right, so she blasted out loud, "To Angela's ass!"

The shots were consumed.

Monica almost coughed it up through a fresh fit of laughter.

Jeff was cute, she thought. He had to drink his shot in two swigs.

"I never saw somebody split up a shot before," Chip said. "I guess the egg heads can't take a drink, huh? Not like us roughnecks."

A silence hung between them.

Chip appeared to be angry.

Jeff was nervous. He gave everybody a deer in the headlights expression. "Look, I don't mean anything by it. I respect your profession. We're all people. We're just...all...fun-loving people trying to make it in life. Yeah. I mean no offense."

Chip reached over and punched his shoulder. "I'm fucking with you, school boy. The look on your face. What'd you say a second ago? 'We're all fun-loving people.' You should've been a philosophy major."

Angela interrupted them again. "The real reason I came here, besides engaging in conversation with the finest people in the history of the world, was to really congratulate Monica. I know the story. Her old boss in New Jersey, Mr. Moody, who is the son of the ex-CEO of Polar Security, grabbed Monica's ass. What does Monica do? She kicks the man in the balls. I mean, the guy went to the hospital. I heard he almost lost one of his testicles. It's too bad he didn't. He threatened to sue her if she didn't take this job out here in Alaska. Now the man's on his way to prison, and Monica's here with us, and her luck has changed.

"I wanted to add, when I was going to a training seminar, I had to deal with Mr. Moody's father. He grabbed my ass when nobody was around. He said some very inappropriate things. I was younger and stupid then. I didn't call him out or do anything about it. Sexual harassment thrives on silence. Monica didn't hesitate to do something about it. She's one tough girl. I barely know you, and I already think the world of you."

Angela got up and gave Monica a hug. "We're happy to have you. No matter what you do in the future, it's been a pleasure."

Ted and Chip pointed at the stage. "The ladies are coming out. Get your dollar bills out!"

"Speaking of sexual harassment," Angela said to Monica. "I'm heading home. I've already had too much to drink."

Monica agreed. "I'm done too."

She paid her tab, leaving a ten on the table.

Bob, Ted, and Chip had already moved closer to the stage. Their night was just beginning. The strippers were walking out onto the stage.

Jeff walked outside with Monica. "Wait. Can I show you something at the work site? If you want to, I mean. It's really cool. We're setting up something that might reveal what my dad's been trying to uncover. He says it'll keep our department in funding for decades. This is huge. I guess Alaska is full of these cool finds. He's proving unconfirmed theories correct after decades of research."

She didn't know what he was talking about. But it still interested her. "Sure. I'd love another look."

"I would drive, but I've had one too many."

"It's only a few blocks," Monica said. "Let's moonlight."

He hooked arms with her. "Okay. Let's moonlight."

Moonlighting tonight would mean total terror.

BLOWN TO SMITHEREENS

Jeff used the platform elevator to reach the bottom of the dig site. The late evening chill managed to halfway sober up Monica. She could talk without stumbling over her words. Jeff wasn't struggling through his words. He was super enthused.

"The science department doesn't fully realize the implications behind the success of this project. My dad can't sleep. He's so excited. I'll admit, he was a bit depressed before now. It looked like this dig site wasn't going to yield anything new. It's like my dad had his fifteen minutes, and they were over before anything really happened.

"It's not over. That I promise you. If we find life forms shifted from other regions of the world behind the rock walls in that cave, it could change how we look at the Big Bang Theory and the extinction of dinosaurs. Imagine if the world completely shifted on it axis, turned inwards, dumped life forms into this region, and they were frozen here in time.

"I've had a good look at the cavemen down there. They're perfectly preserved. A magnificent, worldly event caused this world shifting to occur. I mean, we could be changing history. I mean, wow! This could mean a job for the rest of our lives. Good money. Good work. Serious history making on our part. How badass is that? It's like we're giving a double throat punch to science and history at the same time."

"Settle down," Monica laughed. "You're giddy. That's really cool. I see what you're getting at. So when do you see what else is down there? I mean what's still hidden deeper in the ground. The double throat punch to history stuff?"

"That's what I'm getting at. Allow me to show you."

The elevator arrived at the bottom floor. The work lights were on. Jeff was puzzled by that. "Wait. The work site shouldn't be lit up. Dad gave everybody the night off."

They overheard a couple of people talking in a heated manner. Jeff took the lead. Monica struggled to keep up with him. The ground was slick with ice. Through the earthy tunnel, she trailed behind him. When they reached the site, Monica's stomach sank. She went stiff with fear.

Jeff challenged the intruder. "What the hell are you two doing here?"

Ryan, the guy who asked her for weed the other night, had a 9mm pistol aimed at the evening's security guard. His coat read Gus. Monica hadn't met the older gentlemen who was in his fifties. Gus had his hands up. He relayed the situation to Jeff.

"Your classmate here has decided to try and abscond with your cavemen. He's turned up the space heaters full blast. There's melted water all over the place. This idiot doesn't realize this whole place is an electrical hazard to begin with. None of this is up to code. When I told your buddy here I was going to call the police if he didn't leave, he pulled a gun on me."

"Ryan, what are you doing?" Jeff was beside himself with anger. "You shouldn't be angry. My dad was lenient. He could've kicked you out of the program indefinitely. He gave you a break, and this is what you do in return?"

"Whatever, Jeff. Your father's an asshole. He wants to take credit for the work we've done. We sweat and break our backs while he soaks up the accolades. It's not right. He won't be famous without his precious cavemen. Without the help of his students, he's nothing."

Monica noticed Ryan's body was unstable. He was swaying and rocking. The distraught student was tanked.

"You've been drinking," Monica said. "There's nothing we can't settle by talking it through. Really think about what you're doing here. Nothing good can come out of it."

Gus stood beside her. "There's no point reasoning with the idiot. He's irrational and very, very drunk. He discharged his weapon. The bullet was an inch from hitting me. The kid's lost his marbles. I guess the professor's worked him too hard."

"I'm not putting up with anybody's shit anymore," Ryan growled. "My girlfriend broke up with me today. We were supposed to get married. Then the professor threatens to have me expelled just for asking you for some weed. After working for that asshole for free, and putting in hours I won't get paid for, and busting my ass day in, day out, your dad scolds me like a child. I'm a dedicated student. Forget this shit. You know what? I'm not going to steal these cavemen. You're wrong about that guess. *I'm going to destroy them.*"

Ryan aimed his gun at them with one hand, and he dug into a giant duffel bag and revealed an axe with the other. "Once these guys are soft enough for dismemberment, I'm going to go all slasher-movie style on these assholes. The professor won't have anything to show for his work, and the millions and millions of dollars spent except for Cro-Magnon sushi."

"You've lost it," Jeff shouted. "You're drunk. Stop this. You're upset about a bunch of things. I get it. You can still stop what you're doing and move on from this. You haven't done anything wrong yet. I can talk my dad into fixing everything. He's worked you guys hard. It's because he sees potential in this place. In you, Ryan. In the whole crew. You're one of us. Let me help you get through this bad patch. We're friends, aren't we? We'll sober you up. Get a hot meal in you. Everything will calm down. Things will get better. I promise."

Ryan's eyes softened. He realized he was carrying an axe in one hand and a 9mm in the other. The fact disturbed him. He started blubbering.

"Oh my God, what am I doing? I've been drinking since six in the morning. After Trisha broke up with me, I've been tanked. I've lost my mind. I'm so sorry, Jeff. You two, I'm so sorry. I'm putting down my weapons. You'll help me. You won't kick me off the crew, will you? Promise me you won't."

"I swear to you, Ryan."

"Okay."

Ryan was starting to put down the axe and the gun. He was in tears. The reality of what he was going to do was setting in.

Gus pointed at one of the dozen space heaters. "Stand back!"

Monica saw a pool of water rising up to the space heaters high enough that sparks were starting to blast from the boxes. The electrical box across the room, and the outlets, started to crackle with electricity. Blue branches of electrical currents spread about the room, violently forking in all directions.

Everybody raced out of the room. Monica followed behind, being the last in line. She caught the cavemen standing there, frozen in death. They were being jolted by wicked currents of juice. The room was lit up with blue energy and sparks. Parts of the ceiling broke, caved in, and new sections of the underground lair were revealed as the electricity did its damage.

The electricity reached its peak before the electrical box exploded.

Every light went dark.

The electrical surge left them in pitch darkness. A few battery-powered emergency lights came on, poorly illuminating their surroundings. Stray sparks would pop every few seconds. Monica stood there with the others outside the tunnel. She could feel her heartbeat chugging in her chest. The night's arctic wind gave a nice howl to kill the silence.

Ryan was apologizing under his breath. "I'm so sorry. I destroyed them. I know I did."

"*Shhh*. Quiet. Shut up a second." Gus hushed them. "You hear that?"

"Hear what?" Monica asked.

"It sounds like movement coming from back in that tunnel."

Gus turned on his flashlight. "Better check it out. I'm on duty. Besides, your buddy didn't make it out with us."

Monica gasped. "Jeff is still back there? Oh my God. I thought he made it out. I swore he was in front of me. Everything happened so fast."

"No. He's still in there. I hope he didn't get shocked." Gus pointed the flashlight back towards the tunnel. He called headquarters on his walkie and asked for a police car. "Okay. I'm going in. Help will be on the way soon."

Monica was glued beside him.

Ryan stayed behind. He sobbed to himself. His muttered apologies grew fainter with each forward step.

When Gus's flashlight beam touched the room, Monica let out a blood-curdling scream.

PART THREE: CAVEMAN MASSACRE

CLUBBED

"Run! They're alive. The electricity brought them back to life! I don't know how it's possible. Turn back! *Ahhhhgawwwd!*"

Monica stared on in horror. One of the male caveman, towering at seven feet tall, had Jeff by the neck in one giant hand. The caveman lifted him up with no effort. He was a powerful savage. Those cold eyes only knew hunger and savagery. He was painted an orange color. A couple of sections of the cave had small fires burning, lighting up the cave scene.

Jeff's peals of pain reached their height when the caveman uprooted Jeff's head from his body in one jerk. His death cry was startling. "*Eee-aaaaaagh!*"

His spine was still connected to the uprooted head. The caveman had ripped it off with such incredible force. Two of the cavewomen grabbed Jeff's headless body and went to work. They used stone tools to dismember him. The child savage worked in the background to start a fire by gathering a stick covered in flames. The killer caveman clutched onto Jeff's neck and ate at the raw strips of dangling meat hungrily. Half his face was slathered in blood as he smacked his starving lips together.

"Grab that axe, and hurry," Gus whispered to Monica. He had already picked up the 9mm Ryan had dropped from earlier. "I got the gun. We're going topside. Let's move our feet out of here. Quietly. This is beyond fucked up."

Behind Gus, a caveman had snuck up on him. He had a giant club. The club was skinny at the bottom and really thick at the top. The weapon was rendered over Gus's head. A sickening, skull-cracking WHOMP followed the connection. The night security guard's brains were smashed into his jaw line. The collision was a spray of bone shards and gray matter. Gus's tongue sloshed around in his messy mouth for seconds before collapsing dead.

The caveman reached down and picked through the brains, eating them with vigor. Monica watched the beast man pick up Gus with two giant hands and eat at his head like it was a meat ice cream cone.

These beings had been frozen for millions of years.

Their hunger was insatiable.

Monica stumbled backwards out of the tunnel. She couldn't keep her eyes off of them. They were amazing and terrifying at the same time. The two cave women and the child had Jeff's torso turning on a handcrafted spit. The stench of cooking flesh made her stomach turn.

Got to get out of here before these people eat me.

Every step was made with extreme care. The earth was slick with ice. Each tread was the crunch of snow and shards of frozen earth.

She was in the dark again. She could barely see her hand in front of her face. The dim glow of the firelight down the tunnel shed very little light.

Jeff's dead. Gus is dead.

Those people...are eating them.

They're cannibals.

Nobody's going to believe this.

The police!

I have to get up the stairs and call them.

She quickly remembered Gus had already called them. Help should arrive soon, she thought, with limited reassurance.

Monica was weak with fear. She thought when extreme situations happened like this that the body kick started itself into survival mode. So far, she could barely plant one foot in front of the other. Then she remembered the sounds of so many bones being broken by pure force, and the smacking noises of flesh being eaten raw.

She finally found the ability to move faster again.

Then she stumbled and fell backwards. She let out a great big scream.

"I'm so...so...sorry."

She tripped over a body. "*Ryan!* Come on. Get up. We have to get out of here, and fast."

Ryan's drunk apologies abruptly ended. An arrow slammed into his left eyeball. The orb squirted out a juicy gush of yellow pus. The arrow stuck out the back of his head. Blood leaked out of his skull like a sieve. Three more arrows quickly followed up the first one. Two landed with hard *thwack* sounds into his chest. The third arrow landed between her feet.

Monica's instincts were working full blast. There was no time for eloquent observations or sadness for the fallen dead. Her ass was on the chopping block, and these hungry cavemen were the greedy butchers.

She knew the freight elevator wouldn't work.

The electricity was out.

Monica charged up the scaffolding. Two more arrows shot in her direction. She felt one whiz right by her left ear.

Damn, that was close!

She was a scared streak that could outrun anything in that moment.

The scaffolding winded upwards forever. Monica refused to slow down. They could be upon her at any moment.

What was she going to do? Professor Sterling would have to be notified that not only had his cavemen come to life, but that his son had been brutally murdered and cannibalized.

The police will take care of it.

Gus already called them.

They'll be here any moment. Let the police do their job.

When Monica reached topside, she was out of breath. Seconds later, two policemen had parked in the above parking lot. They approached from the top of the stairs. Soon, they arrived at the site with flashlights casing the area.

She thanked God.

She was safe.

FALSE REASSURANCE

The words came out of Monica's mouth too fast to be easily comprehensible.

"You have to do something. Call more police. They're down there dead. Those things murdered them. Those people, I mean. They're alive. Oh my God, we can't just stand here. We need more police. A S.W.A.T. team. The military. They're dangerous, and they're probably on their way up right now. Why are you staring at me like that? I'm not crazy."

"Ma'am, have you been drinking?"

"That was hours ago. I've sobered up. It was Gus. He works for Polar Security. He called in the distress call. I'm not drunk. Poor Gus. He's dead too."

The two cops gave each other an annoyed glance.

"We'll take you into the station where it's nice and warm. Then, we can hash out what's going on. Sound good?"

"Aren't you going to take a look down there?"

"Professor Sterling has been notified that there's been an incident. He's on his way right now."

"You can't let him go down there alone. Those people are dangerous."

"Who is down there, ma'am?"

Her tongue went rigid. What was she going to tell them? Cavemen had murdered three people? No way.

"Trespassers."

One officer turned her around. "It's clear you're intoxicated. Now let's run you down to the station and talk. I'm freezing my buns off out here."

The other officer was looking around. "Where's Gus? He called this in."

"He's dead, damn it. Why won't you believe me? We're all in danger. They're coming up as we speak. They'll kill you."

"Yeah, right, lady. You're drunk as hell. We tried to be polite about it. Now where's Gus? We want answers. He'll tell us everything."

The officers went quiet. They could hear hard footsteps thump against wood. Each step, the scaffolding gave a sharp cry of protest at the weight of whatever was coming up.

"What did you say was down there?"

Monica stared at the head of the stairs. Any moment, they would appear.

"You want the God's honest truth? You won't believe it."

"Try us."

"They're cavemen."

The cops busted up in nervous laughter. "Of all the things I expected you to say, that was the last. Ma'am, nice try. We're not stupid. We're tired, and cranky, and very very annoyed. Gus wouldn't pull any shenanigans. That means something really fishy is going on. This isn't a college prank, is it?"

"Of course it isn't. I'm not even a student. I moved here like two days ago. What reason would I have to pull some shit? I just got a new job. I know it sounds like utter bullshit. You keep standing there and waiting, and we'll be dead in no time. I'm going to run in the other direction. I suggest you do the same."

"You're not going anywhere except for in the back of our squad car. Stay where you are."

The steps were louder. Monica pointed at the work site entrance. Through the veil of the night, a weak shape formed. She knew it was one of the male cavemen. He had a wooden club in one hand and the fire axe Monica had dropped without realizing it on the way up.

"Hey you, buddy. Who are you? Identify yourself."

"It's one of them!" Monica was violently gesturing towards the squad car. "Let's go. Throw me in the back. Hell, toss me in jail. Just get me out of here. They're going to kill us all. Listen to me, would you?"

Whoosh.

The fire axe fluttered forward at impossible speeds. Thrown so hard, the axe went right through the officer standing closer to her. The axe exploded out between the officer's shoulder blades. The weapon struck the hood of the squad car with a crunch of steel and stuck there.

The other officer wasn't able to process the attack. "Dale! What happened to you?"

The officer stared at his partner who was coughing up blood one moment and was dead on the snow the next.

"Run!" Monica demanded, starting to charge up the hill towards the university. "You can't fight them."

"Like hell I can't!"

The officer withdrew his pistol. He got two shots off before the caveman grabbed him by the neck. He was spun upside down. The caveman had him by the legs.

"Let go of me, you son-of-a-bitch! No! No! *N-ooooooooooo!*"

The caveman yanked his legs in opposite direction and tore him in half. Both halves spurted blood and plopped out organs. More of the cave people lunged from the entrance to fight over long intestines. The tug of war was violent as each one of them gave impish sounds of anger.

"*Gruh.*"

"*Grah.*"

"*Mwah.*"

"*E-gah!*"

Ribs were cracked from the skeleton. The little caveman boy was flensing the ribs of precious and succulent meat. The group was hunched over their kill like a lion would a dead gazelle. Jerking and bobbing of heads indicated wild feasting.

Monica retreated to the police car.

The keys weren't in the ignition.

"*Damn it, damn it, damn it.*"

Panic mode set in. It would be her body next they would be breaking open and filling their bellies with. She crunched through the snow, bolting away from the visceral carnage. She could still hear the wet sounds of teeth flensing meat from bones and fleshy sacks and organs popping open and leaking vital fluids.

Forever disgusted, Monica worked her way up the long uphill steps that would take her to the campus. She wasn't sure who would still be around. Anybody would do. She would settle for a phone even.

There's only six or seven of them. Maybe more. Hell, I don't know.

The police can take care of them. When they see what happened to those poor officers, they'll bring in serious reinforcements.

She created a mental checklist of things to do once she made it into the university. That checklist would soon be useless. She was too shaken up and in a hurry. Monica lost her footing. She stumbled, fell backwards, and with nothing to latch onto for grip, she tumbled down the steps.

She struck her head on the way down.

The blow rendered her unconscious.

ON THE LOOSE

The group of cavemen decided to leave the youngest of their group behind. The child would guard the meat below in the work site. The cave women worked to stack up dismembered arms and legs like cordwood and delivered the pieces below to their home. While they were transporting the pieces, the three cavemen topside gathered in a semi-circle to hatch a plan.

"Hrrrr." *Hungry.*

"Gratch." *Flesh.*

"Yawp." *Store.*

"Che-gah." *Cold.*

"Wrug." *Winter.*

"Hrrrr." *Hungry.*

"Yeagh." *Kill.*

"Gratch." *Flesh.*

"Grrrgh." *Stalk.*

"Grrrgh." *Stalk.*

All together, "Grrrgh." *Stalk. Stalk. Stalk.*

The light snowflakes that had been falling the past few hours turned into thicker and heavier falling precipitation. Monica, landing near the bottom of the stairs, was quickly covered up and was out of sight. When the cave women returned with more weapons, the cavemen relayed their plan to harvest food for the long cold winter.

Together, the cave people hiked up the stairway and made their way on campus.

The flesh harvest was on.

PROFESSOR STERLING

Things were looking up in such a hurry, so of course, it was Professor Sterling's luck something bad would happen at the dig site. He received a call from both Polar Security and the police that there was a disturbance. He was driving against the harder hitting snows. Wintry weather was a beast, and tonight, it was starting to show its teeth.

I knew Ryan was mad I suspended him from work for a few days. I didn't think he would take retribution on the project. I swear, if one hair is missing on a caveman's back because of that kid, I'll kick him out of the program for good.

The professor clutched the wheel tighter. He was proud of himself for putting chains on his tires the other day. He rarely drove. He lived within easy walking distance of the university. This late at night, he wanted to reach the site as quickly as possible to dodge a possible catastrophe.

He parked in the empty university parking lot. The area was silent but for the wintry mix coming down in downy sheets. Visibility was getting more and more diminished by the second. He got out of the car and was whipped by hard-hitting winds. He rushed down the steep concrete stairs at the very back of the university and hurried towards the work site.

When he arrived at the top of the stairs, he noticed the police vehicle half-covered in snow. He noticed the large trails of dripped blood on the snow. He bent down to inspect it closer and found…a human mandible covered in strands of muscle tissue.

Jesus, God in heaven. It looks like someone just ripped this out of someone's mouth!

The professor jerked his head in every direction, thinking an aggressor would lunge out of nowhere and do the same to him.

Who could do this?
I mean...my God.

Whatever it was, the police couldn't handle it. The patrol vehicle's driver's side door was open. There were no keys. He tried his cell phone. He managed to get a signal. His fingers hit 9-1-1. The line rang and rang. Nobody picked up.

What's the meaning of this? Why isn't 9-1-1 picking up?

He heard somebody groan. It was faint up against the screaming winds. The professor saw somebody move in the snow. He ran down the steps. He reached the person and prayed they had some answers for him.

Monica stirred. Her brain felt like somebody had pulled the pin on a grenade and left it in her skull to detonate. There was a sizeable lump on the back of her head. When she came to, she slowly got onto all fours. She couldn't quite get to her feet yet. She shivered against the intense cold. Confusion set in for a string of panicked moments. Then she remembered the savage cavemen. The killings. The cannibalism.

She sprang to her feet anticipating one of the murderous Cro-Magnons to be upon her. There was somebody nearby. She sighed in relief when she could finally tell who it was coming towards her.

"Professor!"

Professor Sterling helped her to her feet. He clutched both of her arms. He was desperate for answers. "What's going on here? The police were here. Where are they now?"

"They're dead."

"Dead? What do you mean? Just what is happening here?"

She had tears in her eyes. "You won't believe me. They killed the police. Your son. I'm so sorry. He didn't make it. Jeff's dead."

"My son is dead?" The words blasted from the professor's lips. "You have some explaining to do. Start talking and making sense."

"You see the blood, don't you? People were slaughtered here. The police are gone because they took the bodies with them."

"They, who?"

"You won't believe me."

"Talk to me, Monica. I'm listening. Believe me, my ears are wide open. If something's happened to Jeff, I want to know everything."

Monica explained the situation about Ryan, the electrical surge, and the cavemen coming to life and slaughtering everybody in sight.

She couldn't read into the professor's stoic expression. He was on pause. He didn't say anything. He raced up the stairs instead.

"Where are you going?"

"I'll be right back. You stay put. Don't move a muscle. We're getting to the bottom of this mess."

"No. It's dangerous. More police are on their way. We should wait for them."

"Don't be so sure, kiddo. I tried calling them. Nobody picked up. We might be on our own."

She blurted out a bunch of questions. The professor ignored her. He marched up the steps against her protests.

"Stay put," was all he said.

She waited for what felt like an hour for the professor. When he returned, he had a flashlight in his hands and a bundle of road flares. He struck two of them and spread them out so the area was a burning green color. She could see the work site entrance again. The dark pit that promised death.

The professor handed her three unlit road flares. "Hold onto these. I take everything you've said to me very seriously. If Jeff's in trouble, I want to help him. You may be stressed, or terrified, or confused about what attacked you guys. I'm not going to make any judgments until I can see for myself what happened."

"Wait. What are you saying?"

"You're going down there with me and checking it out."

WAITING IN THE DARKNESS

"No, I'm not going down there! You haven't seen what's down there. Hear what I'm saying, please."

"It's exactly what you said," the professor insisted. "Until I see what's down there for myself, I can't talk any further about the matter. I'm going down there with our without you. If you care about my son, you'll show me what you're talking about."

She thought about the moment she fled in the opposite direction of the cavemen. Where had they gone? Did they return to the cave? Or did they venture out? She couldn't know until it was too late.

"The police aren't going to help us right now, for whatever reason. I need your help, Monica. Please. It's my son's life we're talking about here."

"The first sign one of those things are coming, we book it out of there. Deal?"

The professor struck a flare. He gave her the flashlight.

"Yes. Deal. Thank you, Monica. Let's get down there. Jeff could be hurt."

He's not hurt. He's dead. Jeff's in pieces. If only you knew!

She didn't want to tell him the straight truth. She was starting to see cracks form underneath the professor's normal stoic facade. The tremors in his voice. The tears forming in his eyes. There were no words to console him. She could only show her support by braving the darkness below with him.

"Remember. The first sign of trouble, we turn back. Deal?"

"Deal," the professor agreed again. "Now let's hurry."

Monica had to double her step to keep up with the professor. Down the scaffolding, the shadows were ever-shifting. The road flare's burning made everything around them dance. She did her best to keep the flashlight in her hand steady. She was trembling everywhere.

The stairs were covered in blood and footprints double the size of a normal human's.

This puzzled the professor. He leaned down and traced his finger around one solid print. "There's no way. No way. This can't be real. It's a prank. It's something other than what it appears to be."

He whirled on her. He shook her by the collar of her coat. He was all gritted teeth and harsh words. "You better not be joking when it comes to my son's life. Now take a moment. Think real nice and hard. You have one more chance to tell me the truth before I do something very bad. Is this one of the students' jokes? Yes or no. Please level with me."

She was about to spit out the answer.

He shushed her. Then he drew his face in closer to hers. The snarl in his face could've been carved with a chisel. "Is this one of the students' jokes?"

Something in her changed in that moment. She was no longer that mistreated girl chewed up and spit out by the legal system. Witnessing someone torn to ribbons and devoured flipped on a switch in her mind.

People were in danger.

She was in danger.

She would help those in need no matter the cost. She was a whole person again, and now, it was time to show some serious character.

What she did next shocked the professor.

She pushed him back. "Don't you lay your hands on me ever again. This is not a joke. Your son is dead. You follow the blood tracks down into that cave, and you'll find your answer there. You want my help, you got it. Otherwise, don't bully me."

The professor really heard what she said this time.

"I'm sorry, Monica. My head is in all directions. My son. He can't be dead."

"I'm sorry. There's nothing we can do about it. Follow me. I can't change what happened. I might be able to save you from what killed Jeff. Those things are either still down there, or they're on the loose. Either way, we have a problem. We'll have to go the police station ourselves and make them aware of what's happening. It shouldn't be too hard. Two of their officers are dead. I watched them die."

This time, she took the lead.

Their steps were sticky and making *schluck* sounds with every new tread. Blood caked the scaffolding.

The professor was beside her now. Fear showed on his face. He was starting to believe things because the evidence was painted red and at their feet.

Another piece of evidence presented itself.

A spear stood upright at an angle in the scaffolding.

The professor bent down to study it. "This wood. It's got to be millions of years old. The stone tip. It's exactly what the cavemen would've used historically. My God. This…is…really…happening."

The professor lunged down the rest of the scaffolding.

"Jeff! Jeff! Are you down there? Son, answer me!"

He was a moving streak, colored by the green burning flare. The crazed man rushed into the tunnel. Once he made it through the other side, the man let out a yell.

"*Ohmygawd!*"

There was something down there with him.

HORROR LURKS

Monica raced after the professor. She was through the tunnel and out the other side in seconds. The cave was painted in fiery-green road flare color. The professor stood there with his mouth agape. The corpses from earlier were stacked by the fire. A torso continued to roast on a spit, kicking out the sickly sweet smell of cooking meat. The area was so thick with the tang of flesh, Monica gagged against it.

Hanging up from the ceiling were coils of thinly sliced meat. Red translucent in color. Guts also dangled from up high. They were squeezed clean of their contents for the purpose of eating. Long shapes of skin were cut. Monica guessed for wearing, the way they were sliced into long cloth-like chunks.

She expected to see the group of cavemen stalk after them. Only one had stayed behind. The youngest of the pack. She had long scraggly and greasy hair. The nasty mop was so long, it went down to her toes. She wore a sash made of animal leather and bottoms that were tatters that barely covered her private parts. The savage didn't care. It used a long stick to work off hunk after hunk of meat from the hot human torso. It tore off a nipple and shoved it into her mouth. It gnawed and chewed with a fervor unknown to Monica's personal history.

"It's really true," the professor said in stunned awe. "They're alive. It makes sense. Look at the bodies behind the girl."

Monica did, reluctantly. Through the glow of orange firelight and the artificial green burning color of the road flare, dismembered pieces were stacked beside the fire in a macabre collection.

"The girl is guarding the food while the adults procure more meat. They're storing for winter. Here, in these climes, they think it's always winter. They'll always be hunting for meat. They're out there right now hunting…oh no. J-Jeff."

Jeff's head was stacked beside the other crudely severed heads.

"He really is dead."

The cave girl gave a hiss at the tearful commotion. *"Hraaaaah!"*

"Shut up, you little brat! My son is gone. You killed him. You savage! All because of my work. He died because of me."

"That's crazy," Monica defended him. "The electricity somehow brought them back to life. You and Jeff had nothing to do with it. Blame Ryan, if you want to blame anybody, and he's dead too. We can't focus on those things now. Jeff would want you to save others from being harmed. Those cavemen are out there, and they're dangerous. He ripped one of those officers in half with his bare hands."

The girl was bent on all fours like a wild feral creature. Teeth were bared into a snarl. Those eyes glinted with beastly intent. She could tear your throat out just for the pleasure of watching someone bleed. She gathered up a spear and brandished it with the intent to chuck their way.

Upset and barely able to talk, the professor cast aside his emotions for a moment. "Monica, I'm lucky to have you here. You're right. Jeff wouldn't want anybody else to die."

"What about the girl?"

"She won't go anywhere."

"How do you know that?"

"She's guarding the food. If we step any closer, she'll throw that spear."

"Then let's go. The police need to be made aware of what's happening. As crazy as it sounds. You can help give credibility to the situation, Professor."

"Hraaaah!"

The cave girl arched her arm back as if to toss the spear. Every muscle in her lean body flexed with incredible power. Her body language warned them that she was a dominant creature, so back off, or die.

Together, they returned topside. Before they reached the stairs to the parking lot, they could feel the ground rumble.

Doom-Doom-Doom-Doom-Doom-Doom-Doom x 500.

She imagined dozens of people with cinder blocks for feet stomping at incredible speeds. It was coming from the bottom of the dig site.

Monica and the professor braced themselves for what was coming their way next.

ESCAPE!

The cave girl stayed close to the fire. She continued to eat off the torso cooking on the spit, selecting the most succulent parts for herself. She dug deeper into the cut open torso and removed the gall bladder and chewed the tasty juices out of it before spitting the chewy hunk out of her mouth. To her, it was like swallowing a piece of rubber. The girl admired the stacks of piled-up bodies. They promised many nourishing meals and survival. They would outlast the harsh winter.

Her sharp stick dug through the bone notches of the torso's sternum. She craved a morsel from the heart. A ventricle would do, or maybe a chamber of the heart. The deeper the meat, she had learned through her instincts and what her parents taught her, the better tasting the meat.

She was working her stick, jabbing, jamming, and poking for what her belly rumbled for when she heard the rock walls behind her shift.

Soot crumbled from the ceiling. When the walls shook, bigger chunks of rocks came loose. The cave girl dodged the rocks, raising her voice in a shrill.

"*Haaaaaagh! Naaaaaargh! Raaaaaatch!*"

The ground in front and behind her collapsed. The collection of human meat tumbled into a deep sinkhole. The girl, too, was pitched downwards when the ground beneath her vanished.

Up from the very icy depths, the electricity had stirred what lay dormant below the earth for millions of years. Out of the darkness and into the firelight, the large group climbed out of their grave and returned to life. The stampede burst up from the ground so fast and so numerous, the cave girl was stamped to death against the vertical incline they rose up from.

With blood on their hooves, the giants came up from the ground to defend the earth.

"Watch out. They're coming right our way!"

Monica shoved the professor away from the stairs to let them through. They both landed in the snow, tripping hard.

Watching what escaped come closer, she couldn't but ask herself: *What the hell are they?*

"Stay down," she kept telling the professor. "They'll knock you down."

The professor was standing in place, unafraid of being harmed. His eyes were deadlocked on them. Mastodons. They were the size of elephants with brown and black brindle hair. Each had two curvy tusks that jutted out long enough to easily gore any opponent.

The ground trembled with each advance of the seven-ton beasts. There were easily a dozen that had charged up the scaffolding to the surface. They bounded up the steps. Their destination was impossible to know.

When they were gone, everything turned to stark silence. Even the snow and winds had calmed.

"I can't believe it. It's like whatever was down there came to life. Electricity did it. Unbelievable. What *else* could be down there?"

"I don't know," Monica said. "And I don't want to know. Are you going to take me to the police station, or what? I know science is happening all over the place, but so is death."

Mentioning death snapped him out of his ruminations.

"Yes. Of course. My car's up top. I'll take you to the station. This is beyond our control."

Together, they made their way up the stairs. The concrete was in broken up shards. They had to tread carefully on the precarious steps.

When they reached the parking lot, both of them stopped.

"Oh," the professor said. "I see."

The mastodon stampede had battered through his vehicle. She imagined the giants stepping on it and flattening it like an empty soda can.

"I guess we're taking it on foot," Monica sighed. "Come on. Let's get to the police station. People are in danger."

Before they made their way through campus, screams of terror could be heard throughout town. She imagined cannibalistic cavemen and the mastodons were causing quite a stir.

"Monica, stop a moment." The professor grabbed her arm. "Look there. It must've snuck out with the mastodons."

She saw it angled on the ground ready to pounce at them.

"Another scientific anomaly! A saber-toothed tiger. That's just great! It's licking its chops. We're meat on a plate to this thing. What do we do?"

"We can't run."

"Then what do we do?"

"Nothing. By the time we take one step, it'll be right on top of us. It's got us in its sights. Maybe you can go one way, and I'll go the other. That way, one of us might escape."

"Yeah, but one of us gets eaten."

"Just throwing out ideas."

"Well, it's a terrible idea."

Monica sized up the threat. It was just like a Bengal tiger…with two giant pointy teeth coming down from its top set of choppers. The tiger was hunched to attack either one of them. Those predator eyes honed in on them. Their meat. Their flesh. The way it kept licking its chops, it was imagining how their insides would taste.

Before she could think through the problem, the professor was running in the other direction yelling for the beast to get him.

"What in God's name are you doing?"

The saber-toothed tiger didn't go for the professor.

It leapt right in her direction with claws protracted and mouth wide open to take the biggest bite.

ON PATROL

Officer George Maker was sitting in his patrol vehicle at one of the town's checkpoints. This was a block away from both local bars. At this time of night, if anybody was driving drunk, he would bust their butts. During the five years he had been an officer here in Fedora, it was a matter of pride catching people in the act, having a brother who was killed by a drunk driver.

He hadn't had much action yet tonight. No reason to turn on his sirens and make chase.

The police frequency suddenly lit up.

"*Distress call down at the university. Two officers down at the dig site.*"

"*Multiple wrecks on 7th Street. Ambulances called onto the scene.*"

"*Man dead on the corner of 9th and Common.*"

"*Partial power outages reported in the residential block of White Hills.*"

Officer Maker whistled.

"The night sure is heating up. What in the heck is going on around here?"

He was about to report in when a problem occurred.

The giant cave man's hand smashed through the driver's window. That powerful grip squeezed his neck so hard it decapitated him.

"*Report in, Officer Maker. We need all the patrol cars to head out to White Hills ASAP. Things are getting hairy.*"

Officer Maker didn't report in.

He was too busy being slit from mouth to groin with a stone axe and sorted for choice meat.

Officer Roberta Marquitz thought she had slid on a patch of ice trying to speed towards White Hills. The disturbance calls kept coming in. People were being assaulted by unknown assailants in their homes.

She was actually spun out by what smashed into her vehicle. Large hulking hairy beasts. Six barreled into the vehicle, treating her car like a pinball. She ricocheted between the mini stampede. When they plowed through her and left her vehicle a useless hunk of junk, Roberta froze. She was now parked precariously on a sidewalk that led into the local grocery store.

All she could say under her breath was, "*Wow. Wow. Wow.*"

She didn't say wow when a cave woman yanked her out of the broken car window by the air, dragging her body against broken glass. The first blow of the thick wooden bludgeon shattered all of her teeth. The second and final blow brained her. The crown of her skull cracked right open. The cave woman dug her dirty fingers into the bloody gray matter and couldn't help but eat every morsel before searching on to sate her next basic instinct.

Procreation.

* * *

Ted Higginbotham heard his wife's screams from the backyard porch. They were east of the White Hills residential community in another suburb. They had no idea about the recent attacks. The sirens just started ringing out from all directions. Linda had let out their bulldog to do his business when the commotion began. Suddenly, Linda was pleading for his help.

He raced out of bed. Ted heard something wet splash against the roof. This wasn't rain. It was like someone dropped hundreds of buckets of water from up high onto the entire neighborhood. New screams multiplied throughout the neighborhood. He was about to open the back door when Linda, on her knees with her hands at her face, beckoned him to stay inside.

"*Don't come outside! It burns. Oh God, it burns! It's like gasoline.*"

Her eyes weren't burning.

Linda's eyes were crying blood.

"I don't care, Linda! I'm helping you."

Ted stomped outside. He reached out to touch her. Her nightgown was sodden in what stank of a weird mix of gasoline, bleach, and ammonia. It stung his eyes to be in such close proximity of her. The fumes, they were noxious.

His hands burned when he touched her. He imagined sticking his hands on the coils of a hot stove. "Oh God! Linda, no!"

He shoved his hands into the snow to cool them off. That seemed to do the trick. He struggled to think of how he could help his wife. She was mewling and suffering, thrashing in place. She too tried to use the snow to help her situation. The warped snow angels were bloody and ill-formed. Soon, her cries of pain ended.

She was dead.

"Linda...Linda, no."

Ted didn't have time to mourn his wife. Up from the night sky, he caught a giant fireball light up the night. The source was from a flying creature. Part dragon, part lizard, it was a bright crimson red color with hideous primeval eyes and an elongated mouth that served as a wild blowtorch. From between its legs, jets of fluids sprayed from its genitals. The wild gush pounded the neighborhood again.

He retreated into his house to avoid the infernal spray.

That's what hit the house. That's what killed Linda.

Dragon piss.

Those outside who came out to investigate the mix of screams and the magnificent creature flying in the sky were doused in urine. They were hit so hard, and there was so much piss, it was a tidal wave that sent people down the street, helplessly caught up in the tide. Once the tide settled, bodies lay in the street, strewn in yards, and on top of snow piles dead.

The smell was starting to get to Ted.

He couldn't stay here.

He kept coughing and blinking tears out of his eyes.

Ted slipped into his winter clothes, boots, and gathered as much of his gun collection hanging from racks on the garage wall as possible. Pump-action shotguns. M-16s. .357 Magnums. Colt

Carbines. Walter PPKs. Long-range rifles. Everything he could strip from the racks in under five minutes, he took along with him.

He opened the garage. The reek of something chemical was so much stronger now. He couldn't stay here. He was horrified by the number of bodies strewn about the block. They were like beached fish on the sand.

It's so horrible.

His cell phone rang. It was Chip.

"You and Linda have to come to headquarters. My God, something's happening that I can even describe. There's something else. It's all over the news. They say there's a monster flying in the sky. It has attacked people all across the world. I still can't believe it. Can you bring any weapons with you? The police aren't going to help us. We're on our own, pal."

"I can't believe it," Ted said. "Linda's dead. I'll explain later. I'm on my way. And yes. I can bring weapons."

Ted was slow to drive out of the neighborhood.

There were bodies everywhere.

Once he was on the road, he drove as fast he could to Polar Security.

Officer Larry Hogue was known for his ability to drive fast in wintry conditions. He was hitting fifty miles an hour when he entered White Hills. He was the first responder to arrive on the scene. The snowcapped houses didn't sit idle in the night like they were supposed to.

Hogue had seen the group of mastodons barrel through the neighborhood. They leveled a series of power lines. Those power lines came right down, the beasts knocking them with the ease of barreling through a 2x4. The live lines were whipping back and forth, jolting anything it touched and casing it in flames. Half the homes were ablaze.

The mastodons were gone, running in the direction in a collective retreat.

What were they running from?

Mr. Henderson, the hardware store owner in town, was charging out of his house completely covered in flames. He wasn't screaming because his skin was burning. He was screaming because there was a giant gash in his stomach, and a giant cave-man-looking attacker had a hold of his intestines. They were unspooling as Mr. Henderson created more distance from the attacker until the intestines ran out of length. He was jerked backwards when that happened. The man was dead from shock when he struck the ground.

Through windows and busted open doors, Hogue watched in jaw-dropping horror as cavemen bashed, speared, sliced, and brutalized people. In the middle of one of the streets, the dismembered pieces of thirty people were stacked. A cave woman threw four heads and one hundred pounds of guts onto the growing pile.

Full of rage and disgust, Hogue drove towards the neighborhood.

The sight high up in the sky distracted him. *"Holy shit. What the fuck is that?"*

The flying creature was magnificent in its size, wingspan, and design. Things like this were supposed to be extinct, he thought. Things like this were supposed to be impossible.

Hogue lost all focus. He had his neck craned up, trying to take in the airborne monstrosity. He crashed right into the fire truck approaching the neighborhood. Both exploded into flames. Those in distress would remain in distress.

What else did a rented house full of single, male college students do on a night like this? Play quarters, Paul Wooster decided with his four buddies. Quarters advanced to beer pong. Beer pong accelerated into ordering several pizzas and busting out hilariously bad B-movies.

Paul was waiting on the couch for the food to arrive. He couldn't wait to put cheese and grease in his stomach. He anticipated a knock on the door any moment.

It wasn't a knock that got his attention.

"Whoa, dude, you gotta see this crazy lady on your doorstep!" Chad parted the living room curtain when he had heard the noise outside. "She's like...a cave girl."

"A girl is all I needed to hear," Danny whooped, spilling some of his beer onto his shirt. "Let her in! I'm tired of this sausage fest. I'd even settled for Brad's sister."

Brad did a push up towards the ground and grabbed a shot glass with his mouth and downed it. "If I wasn't exercising, I'd take that personally. There's not a damn thing wrong with my sister."

"Yeah, you'd bang her, wouldn't you?"

Before the argument could turn into one of their classic drag out wrestling matches, the front door was wrenched off of its hinges by four wild blows. BANG. BANG. BANG. BANG.

The door collapsed into ravaged pieces.

The four college students didn't have a chance. The cave woman, smelling of blood, guts, wet pelts, leather, and body stench, seized Brad. He only weighed one hundred and thirty pounds. She lifted him up by the arm and neck as if testing his weight.

"*Grug-uh.*"

She speared him hard into the coffee table. The fixture split in half just like Brad's skull. He was jittering and spasming for ten seconds before going still.

"I'm calling the police," Danny shouted, picking up the phone. "Oh no! There's no dial tone."

"Don't tell her that!" Paul growled. He fled into the kitchen and grabbed a knife. The cave woman seized his hand and squeezed it. Every bone in his fist shattered. "*Ah-gaaaaaaawd!*"

Paul crumbled to the floor. Simultaneously, Danny was manhandled. The cave girl squeezed Danny's arms and legs, testing the limbs for size and power. The Cro-Magnon was quickly disappointed. She slammed her wooden club across his head so hard it decapitated him and pitched that head through the window and into the backyard.

Chad picked up the knife Paul had dropped previously. "I'm going to cut this cave bitch. You don't hurt my friends!"

The cave woman noticed the ankle brace from when Chad had fallen down a set of slick stairs back at the university two weeks ago.

"*Gruh-uh.*"

Chad lunged at the cave woman. She grabbed his arm, unlocked the bone from the socket, and gave it a great yank. The arm ripped from the body with the sound of someone stretching a length from a roll of duct tape. The severed arm still clutched the kitchen knife. The cave woman used that arm to stab him in the neck four times.

That left Paul laying there helpless with a limp hand.

He was in excruciating pain.

"What are you going to do to me? Please. Don't hurt me. What do you want with me?"

The cave woman wanted to mate. Instinct demanded her to procreate with the best specimen available.

Paul served as that specimen.

She stripped him of his clothing. By the time she had her seed, Paul was left battered with twelve different bones broken, a severe case of whiplash, and what killed him, internal decapitation.

The cave woman stomped out of the house to find more fine specimens to mate with.

SAVED BY THE SEMI-AUTOMATIC

Boom! Boom! Boom!

The staccato burst of gunfire punched enough holes into the lunging saber-toothed tiger to bring it down. Monica looked up at the pick-up truck that had pulled up at the critical moment. There was Chip at the wheel. Ted was in the back, clutching a smoking Walter PPK. His eyes were alight with a mix of excitement and astonishment.

"I always wanted to use my guns outside of target practice. I didn't want it to be because something's killing everybody."

Angela was inside the truck with Bob Berger. They were a mix of on-duty security and off-duty in street clothes.

"Come with us," Chip said. "Hop in the back."

"We were going to go to the police station," Monica said. "Can you take us there?"

"What a coincidence," Ted said. "We were going there ourselves."

She stopped by the professor who was leaning over the remains of the saber-toothed tiger in study. "We gotta go, Professor."

She forced the professor over to the truck. He was still wanting to study the dead creature. Once in the back cab, they were crammed in there tight. Monica looked at Ted, the only person in the back of the truck. He served as protection with his M-16.

"What's happening out there?"

Ted's eyes stayed on their surroundings. "Chaos. Anarchy. Saying it sounds ridiculous. One neighborhood was attacked by a bunch of cavemen. Another neighborhood, my neighborhood, was...well, how else do I say it? Some flying creature in the sky pissed on our houses and killed everybody. Don't ask me why or how. It just happened. Now I'm in this truck hoping to save some lives. It's all that keeps me from losing my mind."

They were quiet after that. The professor stayed in his head. She imagined he was thinking about his dead son. Ted kept scouting the area as Chip drove them to the police station.

What did she have to think about?

Her life had taken so many wild turns in such a short period of time. She moved from New Jersey to Alaska against her will. She was blackmailed into signing an illegitimate contract to work here for a year. Then Mr. Moody was sued, and she was exonerated. That feeling of liberation abruptly changed when prehistoric beasts came alive and slaughtered people right in front of her.

Nothing about the past mattered anymore.

What mattered was doing the right thing. Saving lives and somehow surviving in the process. This event was bigger than herself. Her life problems seemed nothing up against this life shattering event.

Nothing would hold her back in life ever again. She could be a doctor, a lawyer, a surgeon, anything. All the years she spent feeling sorry for herself seemed like such a waste. She would make up for lost time. She vowed it.

All she had to do was live through the night.

Little did she know, the night's horrors were only beginning. She would require more than life affirmations and introspection to save her skin.

FIREBALL ASSAULT

Pockets of town rang out with emergency vehicle sirens. Monica could smell and hear the sounds of crackling fire spread. The residential areas could be seen burning in wild plumes of orange. They were two blocks from arriving at the police station when there was another disturbance.

"Watch out!" Monica shouted. She beat her fist against the back window of the truck. "Chip! Pull to the side. Hurry!"

The pack of mastodons was rushing down the street. They were starting to spread out. The group charged forward in a frantic free-for-all. They bashed through parking meters and stomped the sidewalk into brittle pieces. A couple of cars left parked in front of shops, they climbed over, smashing all the windows, popping tires, and leaving the vehicles totaled. Their collective pounding jostled the ground so hard shop windows along the strip shattered in unison.

"What are those things?" Ted asked. "I've never seen anything like that in my life."

The professor pointed at the sky. "They're being hunted. Look up in the air!"

"Shit! What the fuck is that?" Ted raised his M-16 and emptied an entire clip blasting the sky. "Burn rubber! Forget it. My bullets are useless against it."

The giant red-plated beast kept shooting literal balls of fire towards the mastodons. One of the mastodons was enveloped in flames. Its screams were shrill and harsh on the ears. Monica could feel its agony as its skin was charred black.

A talon-tipped hand reached and picked up the burning animal and dropped it into his hungry mouth. Each chomp was a bone-shattering *crunch-crunch-crunch*. The sound of the flying monster gulping down the red-hot morsel of food shook the town.

The other mastodons sensed their impending doom and doubled their speed.

Chip shouted back at them from the driver's seat. "Hold on! I'm getting us the hell out of here!"

He had to jerk the wheel to the left. The car jumped the curb. A mastodon broadsided them, sending them at an awkward angle right through the already busted-out window of the hardware store.

Three individual fireballs ripped free. Two of them collided into the street, causing broken-up shards to fly everywhere. Another fireball in the shape of a giant soccer ball struck another mastodon so hard it burst through its backside and out its mouth. It tumbled down, coming undone from the inside out in bubbling, scorched pieces.

The dragon flew low, its wings shearing off the top of buildings. The sky was raining chunks of architecture. The monster's scream pierced their ears as death warnings.

It was clear.

They had to move their asses or get turned into pulp.

Monica ducked and avoided a broken brick to the face. The professor had a piece of building scrape the top of his head in a thin line. A line of blood split his awestruck face. Several pieces smashed off the back exhaust of the truck. They were half inside the hardware store and half on the outside sidewalk.

"Get in the hardware store!" Chip said, waving them in. Angela, Ted, the professor, Bob, and Monica ran for their lives. "Move it!"

Bob was the slowest getting inside. Fireball reached down and poked him through the back with his talon. The poor man was gored through, thrashing on the claw and balanced there. Fireball eyed the flailing, bleeding human, with nothing but culinary interest. Fireball flung Bob off the tip of his claw. The man was wailing in pain and horror in mid-air. The force of the throw forced him to do front flips. The motion broke his spine. His cries abruptly ended. No longer moaning in agony, Fireball let Bob's corpse flop onto the street uneaten. Fireball wanted live, wailing, bleeding, horrified prey on its tongue.

Monica couldn't believe Bob was dead. She hurried into the hardware store for protection. Once everybody was safely inside, Monica saw how a pickaxe had been lodged into the engine block of the truck. It must've fallen off of a rack during the crash and pierced the hood. The engine was hissing and leaking fluids. Their mode of transportation was ruined.

"Get away from the truck and the windows," Chip said. "That thing still might try and get into the building. Stay out of sight."

They hunkered down behind a row of cashier stations. The screaming wail of yet another mastodon being cooked rang out.

The professor was speaking out loud. He didn't care who listened. He was so fascinated with the living history, even if it could kill them. "Whatever that was in the sky, it's hunting the mastodons. It could only be one thing. I've read enough texts to venture a guess. It's a predator of the sky. We're talking dinosaur times."

The stomping of the mastodons went quiet.

The dragon was long gone.

"Stuff the egghead bullshit," Ted said. "I really don't care about any of it. We can study the hell out of it when people aren't in danger anymore. For now, we're going to the police station. My truck's totaled. It's not helping anybody anymore. The police are our only option. I want to know what the fuck is going on. I think everybody's had their fill of unbelievable shit. To the police station. Agreed?"

Nobody disagreed.

The group headed down the two decimated blocks to the police station on foot.

MASSACRE STATION

They completed the short walk to the station. Monica's jaw dropped at the sight of blood painting what should've been a safe place. It wasn't a few drops of blood. The walls and floor were glazed. The glass front window of the police window was shattered. Red spatters glistened among the broken shards of glass on the sidewalk. It looked like giant footprints were embedded in the snow surrounding the station. Lines in the snow showed where a body had been dragged to the alley. Monica didn't want to see what had happened to the poor victim. She had already seen enough gore and guts to match a solider in battle.

Ted reloaded his M-16. "It has to be more of those caveman people who did this. God, they're savages. Who wants to check inside with me? We have to know if it's clear."

"We all go together," Chip suggested. "It's the best way."

"Fine with me," Monica said. "As long as I'm not alone."

Angela was sickened when she stepped on something wet that made an uncouth squish. A human brain was split in two halves on the sidewalk. It broke open even wider under the force of her boot.

"I'm going to be sick." Angela lost it, vomiting twice. "It's so disgusting. I can smell it too."

The professor helped her up. "Stay with me. Try not to think about it."

"But brains are all over my shoes," Angela complained, wiping her shoes on the snow. "Disgusting."

Inside the station wasn't much better. It was a literal massacre. The front area was slathered in thick slashes of blood. Chairs were strewn on the tiles, many broken. Monica detected more of those giant caveman prints stamped into the red.

Somebody had punched through the glass pane between the receptionist booth and the waiting area. Monica could see where someone had dragged the poor woman out and smashed her into the floor. Parts of the tiles were broken. Articles of clothing were spread out in strips. A torso without limbs and a head looked to have been pulled open by hand. Nothing remained inside the hollowed-out shell. Eaten empty.

"Is anybody here?" Monica called out. "Anybody? We won't hurt you."

The restricted access door was wide open and almost off of its hinges. Shell casings covered the floor. Bullet holes riddled the walls from .28 caliber to full out 12-gauge blasts.

"The caveman got to them," Ted said with venom. "They've massacred this town. The merciless killers. If I see another one of them, I'm going to send them straight to hell where they belong. I won't hesitate to shoot them dead."

The professor got a call on his cell phone. "Oh, thank God. It's my wife. She's on her way. Great. What a relief. She's alive. And we'll have a car. We can get out of here together. Oh, that's wonderful."

"Maybe," Chip said doubtfully. "I'm not sure if this town isn't on lockdown by now. Judging by the attacks, military will be swarming this place. Any second, we'll be hearing air attacks. Rockets exploding. The works. Besides, you got that fire-breathing asshole on the rampage in the sky. Nowhere is safe."

"You're right," the professor agreed, horrified. "I pray she gets here safely. I almost forgot about that monster in the sky."

"My wife died earlier," Ted said. "At least you have hope the person you love the most could survive. I've got nobody."

"I've already lost my son tonight," the professor argued. "Everybody here is in danger of losing something, if not everything, they love. I pray they don't take my Helena from me. She's all that I have left. I do have something to lose. You know nothing about me."

Talk of loss and heartache ended. They entered the police officer's quarters. Bodies were spread out everywhere. One cop looked to have been grabbed by the legs and slammed into the floor until his head burst. A hand chewed up at the wrist gripped a telephone at one desk. Body parts were hung up from the ceiling fans by coils of guts as if left to dry out like jerky. Monica was hit on the back of the head by a dangling leg. Wet thigh meat slickened her hair.

"Oh, that's nasty!"

Many of the officers' bodies were consolidated for storage. Four torsos without arms, legs, or heads had their ribs and sternums removed. The hollowed-out area was filled with the guts of over a dozen persons. They were like loaded baked potatoes ready for the oven.

"They didn't stand a chance," remarked the professor, startled when he stepped on an eyeball, and it popped. "The cavemen easily overpower us humans. They're ten times as strong as we are. It would take a lot of bullets to bring them down. They're human beasts. I guess we evolved into something a little more compact and emotionally driven."

Monica gasped at the sight of an officer's desk. Seven heads were lined up one beside the other. Long strands of pink muscle meat jutted out of the neck stumps. The skulls were removed to reveal glistening brains. Tongues were yanked out of mouths and spread out alongside the heads for later sorting.

"Cavemen often resorted to cannibalism," the professor provided. "When the long harsh winters dragged on much longer than normal, their stored food supplies were depleted. The weakest of the family were sacrificed first. Tongues and brains were delicacies. The guts were staples of their diet. They never liked the flesh on feet. You see many cavemen dig sites, and you discover a lot of discarded foot bones in large piles next to where they defecate."

"Real nice," Ted griped. "Thanks for the history lesson. Stuff it, egghead. It's sickening."

"Yeah, can it," Chip seconded. "This station's already a horror buffet. Angela's tossed her cookies. Anyone of us could be next to lose their lunch. Lucky for the cold, these remains haven't turned yet. I would throw up if this mess was ripe. Good thing we're not in Cancun, and it's spring break."

The professor didn't understand why the group didn't want the information. Monica understood he was purely being scientific to contribute to the group's survival hopes. The professor let it go, though he sulked for a few moments.

There wasn't much left of the building to inspect. Monica feared there wasn't a single cop left alive.

Everything changed in a blink.

"Everybody freeze!"

The group spun around to discover a gun pointed right at them.

SURVIVOR

"Identify yourselves!"

The officer was a younger man with the name Clarkson on his beige breast pocket. He had a Desert Eagle pistol aimed at them. Fear downgraded what should've been firm authority. The back of his sandy brown hair was wet with blood.

"Son, you're confused," Ted said. "You know us, Billy. Judging by the blood on the back of your head, somebody conked you a good one. You should let one of us take a look at it. It could need stitches."

Billy's eyes softened. He lowered the gun. "Sorry, guys. Yes. I know you. I'm so jumpy. I did take a good knock to the skull earlier."

"What happened here?" Chip asked. "It was the cavemen, right?"

"I'll say it even though I can't believe it's true. Yes. Cavemen. They charged into the station, smashing and pulverizing everybody in sight. They mauled everybody. All I remember is blasting my gun. One of them threw me across the room. I must've been knocked unconscious. I woke up, and, and it was over."

A female screech rang off the walls. Then the pounding of fists. The drum sound rocked the walls.

"What the hell was that?" Ted demanded. "Don't tell me…"

"Yes. When I came to, the cavemen were gone. Except for one. One of the females were sniffing around the cells. She entered one that was open. I shut it behind her. Oh man, she was pissed."

The woman unleashed another screech.

"*Yaaaaaaaaaarp!*"

"*Yaaaaaaaaaarp!*"

"*Yaaaaaaaaaarp!*"

"Can anybody shut her up?" Ted rubbed at his ears. "That's freakin' loud."

"What is she doing?" Monica asked. "It sounds so pained."

Billy didn't have any answers. He shrugged his shoulders. "All I know is it's really annoying. She's been doing that off and on every five minutes, or so."

"We should blast her to pieces," Ted said. "They're murdering everybody. Her being alive isn't doing anybody any favors."

Chip agreed. "Yeah. Why keep her alive? It serves no purpose."

The professor spoke up. "I know what she's doing."

"Oh yeah, what?" Ted challenged. "Is she saying how good we taste? Or what part of our bodies is the most enjoyable to eat?"

"No."

"Then what is she saying," Monica asked seriously. "You know your stuff. I trust you."

"Her cries…are an S.O.S. to the other cavemen. Chances are, the group is on their way here to help her. They'll be here any minute."

Billy's face visibly shook. "Oh shit. We're dead."

Right when the professor said that, they heard a car honk outside.

"Helena!"

The professor rushed to the front of the police station to meet his wife.

The happy reunion would quickly turn into horror.

HARD BATTLE

Monica hurried outside to catch up with the professor. "Wait up. Don't go out there alone. Professor!"

Before they both were outside again, she noticed the car wasn't honking anymore. Screams rang out, accompanied by the shattering of glass. Monica watched the cavemen each grab a hold of the vehicle.

"Helena!"

Monica tackled the professor. "Duck, for God's sake!"

The cavemen had lifted up the car and threw it in their direction. The front end of the small SUV crashed into the police station's already destroyed front area. The vehicle was instantly engulfed in flames. Helena's screams rang out, piercing and horrible. Another explosion of the vehicle, the screams stopped altogether.

"No, Helena!"

The professor tried to run to the station. The cavemen had already stomped their way towards them.

"We need to move, Professor. We're on our own. You can't help her."

The front of the police station was blocked and burning. There wasn't any help coming from anywhere. The professor stared at the burning vehicle where his wife died. His gaze burned with fury.

"My son. Now my wife. I can't take anymore!"

The professor clutched the pickaxe he had carried all this time and lunged towards the group of cavemen. "*Raaaaaaaaah!*"

"Professor, no! What are you doing? We need to run away from them."

The professor got halfway towards them when he stumbled over the broken-up road and smacked awkwardly into the pavement.

Damn it. That man is going to get himself killed.

Monica couldn't let him be brutally murdered.

Fuck it.

She had grabbed an axe back at the hardware store. She didn't want to go anywhere near them. Monica flung if forward as hard and fast as she could muster. The nervous energy of being terrorized all night was channeled into the amazing throw. The meat of the axe smacked right into the male caveman at the front of the group. The blow split his head in two halves. Both sides sloughed off wet and soft.

Monica helped the professor up to his feet. Another male caveman was raising his thick wooden club. He was seconds from crushing the professor's skull when Monica grabbed the pickaxe and jammed it between his legs. The tip pierced through his nut sack and up his ass. Blood flowed in thick spurting gouts down its legs. The barbarian let out a wild yawp of pain and landed hard on the ground, desperately trying to remove the pickaxe.

That left two cavemen.

One male.

One female.

She had no weapon.

"Run the other way, Professor!"

They kept stumbling over the broken-up street from Fireball's earlier attack. The cavemen were nearly upon them. Giant powerful hands reached out to crush, kill, and disembowel. By the end of the attack, these mongrels would both eat and wear their flesh.

Ted shouted at them. "Hit the pavement! Go back to The Stone Age!"

Ted unloaded an entire magazine from his M-16. Every bullet pounded the caveman's skull and chest. Monica watched the historical menace's flesh, bone, and brains disintegrate with each new hot bullet that shredded home.

The group had escaped the station through the back way because the front was burning. Billy was about to address the group when everybody saw her approach. The cave woman from the jail cell had escaped. Her hands were bloody from prying back the metal bars. The angry woman grabbed Billy with two hands by the head. She lifted him up off the ground and tore him like a piece of paper in two.

"Je-sus! Look out!" Chip pointed up at the sky. "It's coming back!"

Fireball flew down low and unleashed four staccato balls of flaming destruction. One pounded directly into the cave woman's torso, throwing her up into the air. By the time she hit the ground, the super-hot flames had already reduced her to a pile of charcoal.

Down the entire block, flames were streaming upwards as if produced from psycho burner jets. Monica and the professor had to leap out of the way to avoid being turned into flame-broiled hamburger.

Angela didn't fare so well. She had tripped against a break in the road. A flaming ball hit her dead on. The orange ate her up and left a black skeleton in its place.

Monica's left foot was on fire. She shoved it into the snow to extinguish the burning. Everybody regrouped. Monica, Chip, Ted, and the professor stayed in front of the post office. They stayed low, hunkering close.

Two mastodons were stomping back towards the university. They were retreating from Fireball. The creature had no problem catching up to them. The four of them watched in awe as the dragon's stomach opened like a sideways mouth. An invisible force of gravity sucked up the mastodons off of their feet. A wicked crunch echoed as the teeth inside of its torso mouth chomped up bones and reduced them to digestible materials.

The dragon was finished eating. It arced its body and touched down on top of the university. The beast's wings were outspread. Throwing back its head, fountains of fire blasted from its mouth. The flames licked away the black from the night sky. After the flames ended, a deafening shriek-call blasted from its mouth. Everybody covered their ears against the grating noise.

When the long call ended, Monica could see new flickers of firelight in the distance. Hundreds of strange flickering motions.

She imagined many people holding up candles. They were coming from pockets of both residential neighborhoods.

Whatever they were, they were headed straight towards them.

FIRE ZOMBIES

Fire trucks, police vehicles, and ambulances had all been prevented from helping those in need. Some had crashed dodging the fire-breathing thing in the sky. Others had been pelted by Fireball's urine and rendered incapacitated. Those incapacitated were awoken by the infernal roar of the sky beast.

They weren't dead.

They were waiting to be reborn.

When those affected by the monster's urine heard the monster's piercing call hit the sky, their collective eyes bulged open. Each of their eyes was forced out of their sockets by twitching, pulsing pink eye socket tissue. That tissue had reformed itself into special fire spouts.

They rose collectively. Standing there for a moment, they waited for that kick-start to march. Fireball flew over them and spat out a thinly veiled blanket of flames. This acted as a pilot light to ignite their strange contamination.

Everybody's eyes became burner jets. Flames spat for several feet in front of them intermittently. Between spits, their eyes would burn on low.

The citizens, now fire zombies, growled and raged to destroy all life. They had no notion of their former selves. They marched on collectively with only one goal. Bathe the living in flames. Cook flesh. Burn everything down to nothing. Scorch the earth.

Their need to douse the world in flames couldn't be abated. Houses, trees, the roads, power lines, anything in sight was doused in flames. New fountains were produced from their bodies the longer their eyes burned. Fingertips melted off for new spouts to spit orange. Persons chewed off their tongues and spit them out to create yet more spouts of flames to explode forth.

The hundreds forged down the road and headed right for where the survivors stood.

BENEATH THE EARTH

The burning screams of the baby mastodons rocked the night air. Each and every surviving baby had been torched, eaten, and destroyed by Fireball. Beneath the work sight behind Alaska University and where the cavemen had escaped, a hole gaped wide open by all the recent shifting of the earth. The electrical surge that had brought back to life the cavemen and the mastodons had tunneled even deeper into the earth. Another life form had stirred awake by the shock. The sleeping giant was no longer asleep.

The ice grave encasing the enormous beast was gradually breaking. New forks and gaps in the earth formed. The constant motion occurring topside was creating much-needed footholds for escape.

The pained cries of the mother's babies reached this parent's ears. The Mega Mastodon, a genetic abnormality, finally opened its eyes. It was ten times as large as any mastodon of its time. A hulking giant. A prehistoric powerhouse. Anger coursed through its giant body. Perfectly preserved, and charged with enough volts of electricity to bring it back to life, this beast was ready to kick some ass.

The sounds of its babies running in terror. The crunching of bones. The devouring of its only living spawn. Each item worked to enrage the beast.

Fireball had destroyed its babies only to piss it off. The dragon taunted Mega Mastodon from its slumber to fight. Fireball knew this special Mastodon was the only worthy opponent on the face of the earth.

They would do battle.

And only one would be victorious.

The earth shifted again.

It was only a matter of time before Mega Mastodon would break free.

SIEGE

Ted didn't waste any time making decisions. He guided them back to the hardware store. There, they each claimed the guns Ted had brought with him from back home. He also grabbed a pair of binoculars. When he scouted the horizon with them, the man's face went deathly pale. He couldn't force himself to tell them what he spied coming on the horizon. The sight was…indescribable.

The others were also afraid to find out what was incoming. Monica couldn't stand being helpless. She was all-to-familiar with that feeling BEFORE this attack broke out.

She stole the binoculars from Ted. "Let me take a look."

"Honey, I don't know if you want to do that."

"I'll decide that for myself."

She saw the horde approaching. Hundreds upon hundreds were marching in a thick mob. That part was the easiest to take in. The rest of it was so bizarre.

The flames, she kept thinking. *My God, the flames.*

Thin and high-pressured spouts of orange and red were spraying from eyeballs, mouths, nostrils, and even fingertips. Around the edges of where flames sprayed, flesh was blackened, popping, and being cooked.

Monica mustered the words and told them what was happening. Everybody had to take a look for themselves to believe it. Once the power of observation overcame disbelief, the group collectively worked to figure things out.

Chip was the first to speak about it. "That flying thing caused this. It pissed on everybody."

"Yeah, pissed on us," Ted said. "The sick fucker. It killed my wife. Whatever was in that mess, it made my eyes burn and my skin itch. They're…infected. Whatever it is, it's making them spit fire like that flying thing."

Chip scratched his head. "They're burning everything in sight. When they get here, they're going to do the same to us."

"Maybe, maybe not," Ted suggested. "We know nothing about what they're doing. And where did that flying thing go?"

The professor finally spoke up. "We got about an hour before they get here and turn this place into a fire sale."

A new voice joined the conversation.

"Phones don't work. Police are on break permanently. The national government is busy fighting other problems. Everywhere, the world is being attacked. Sounds like a perfect time for a drink, wouldn't you say?"

"Deb!" Chip and Ted turned and ran to her. "Where's Bo?"

Deb's eyes teared up. "Those cavemen got him. They ganged up on him. He saved me. I'm alive because of him. God bless him."

Monica hugged Deb to console her. Chip and Ted were talking over their next move. Monica could tell their conversation wasn't getting too far.

They could drive out of town. Fireball would show up. They could lay low and hide. The fire zombies were on their way. They didn't know if the zombies were smart, or if they only walked around engulfing everything in flames. Did they hunt people, or were they mindless destroyers?

The professor was still studying the advanced beings with the binoculars. He made a conclusion. "They'll only have a life for so long. If we can avoid them for another hour or two, we should be fine. Whatever contamination that has affected them will eventually cook their bodies to the point it'll incapacitate them. It's an amazing thing they're going through. How it's possible…it'll take some serious science to master."

"Screw science," Deb said. "I don't want them to cook me. End of story."

"Maybe we should lay low," Ted decided. "We can hide in Deb's club. We'll barricade the stairs leading into the apartment and strip club. We'll turn out all the lights and stay quiet. How about it, everybody?"

Nobody disagreed.

They hurried inside and began the task of securing the entrances.

MOMENT OF CALM

After barricading the lower level stairway to Deb's Debutante's with chairs and tables, they secured the stairway upstairs with more tables and chairs. Monica locked the apartment entrance doors. She ran upstairs and grabbed her cell phone. When she brought it down, she called her parents. They answered on the first ring.

Her mother was frantic. "Monica. You're alive! Thank God. You have to seek shelter. It's coming right for you."

"What is?" She had many things coming for her all night. "It's been insane around here. I'm very lucky to have survived this long, the way things are."

Her mother remained scared. "We've avoided the monster. Many cities haven't. It's all over the news. I mean, the monster is everywhere. The news call it Fireball."

Monica described the flying red dragon.

"Yeah. That's it! You've seen it?"

"Unfortunately, it's here."

"I'm praying for you."

The cell phone signal died. Monica tried calling her mother again. There were no bars. She considered herself lucky to know her parents were safe and out of harm's way.

Deb was serving everybody top-shelf drinks. Anything anybody wanted. Monica could tell the poor woman was doing anything to occupy her mind from tonight's horrors.

Monica asked for water.

She didn't want her senses slowed down.

Chip and Ted were keeping watch outside by the front entrance door. They threw back their shots and smoked a cigarette.

Deb brought out her laptop computer. She kept trying to get an Internet signal.

"The web's been down ever since Fireball showed up. There were all kinds of news reports. It's attacked many countries. Millions killed. I guess it can transport itself from place to place at will. Even halfway across the world, if it wants. Apparently, our flaming asshole monster has friends. Other monsters have been reported attacking random places too."

Monica found that curious. "That's strange. Why would the monster jump from place to place and attack, and then stay here? It's been here for half the night. What's here that's so special?"

"I don't know." Deb shrugged. "But I wish it would leave."

"It's not inclined to do so," the professor said. "I'm guessing there's something here that it wants. It has to do with our dig site. Call it a feeling. Remember when we found the body of the Glyptodon here? The paleontology community flipped out over it. There must be something else under the ground that monster wants. If I were to judge by how those mastodons and cavemen came to life, there must be something alive under the earth Fireball wants. I wish I knew what it was."

"Fireball can go sit on a dildo made of dynamite for all I care," Deb cracked. "Who cares what the monster wants? As long as that thing somehow dies, I couldn't give a damn. Where's our army? We're America. That flying fuck should be mincemeat by now. I understand we're under attack, but come on. I've paid taxes for decades. Uncle Sam sure doesn't mind showing up on payday. But when it's time for HIM to work, he's a no show. Where's our help? Seriously."

Monica understood Deb's anger. She was young and her limited world experiences were full of bitterness and disillusionment. But now something much more important was affecting everybody's lives. She suddenly came to a conclusion.

This was beyond waiting things out.

No army was going to show up and support them.

"We're going to have to help ourselves. Even if it means taking on that monster ourselves."

Everybody went quiet.

Things could be heard moving outside.

MELTING THE ICE

Fireball hovered over the land surrounding the dig site. The beast knew its opponent was under the ground and alive. The only creature on earth that could rival its power stirred. Fireball craved conquest. Its primordial ego wanted Mega Mastodon's death to be painful and dragged out. Then nothing could stop Fireball from world domination.

The monster decided to help its foe from its icy prison.

It wanted Mega Mastodon's demise enough to hurry up its return to life.

Inhaling air and giving life to the flames lunging up its throat, the giant unleashed ten fireballs in burning succession. Sections of the earth succumbed to the hot impact of high-speed flames. The earth forked and broke open. Ten more fireballs, one after the other, the night was alive with walls and walls of orange heat. Blankets of flames bored into the ice, reducing what was once frozen solid earth to liquid.

Off in the far distance, Fireball sensed new enemies on their way. High up in the sky, military air fighters would arrive soon. They would interfere with Fireball's one-on-one battle. The monster needed to keep the human forces occupied.

Fireball's friends were suspended in a space/time flux. He could summon them at will or put them on hold. He was their master, and it could command them at will.

The beast watched the fire-scorched stretch of land burn. The earth visibly shifted. Mega Mastodon was on its way to the surface. Any moment, the magnificent giant would arise.

Fireball hovered in the sky and spread its wings. The nuclear energy pulsing through its body came to surface. Neon green lightning branches crackled across its enormity. Fireball threw its head back and unleashed a wild battle cry. Lightning branches burst from its body in all directions. Unnatural currents of electricity served as crushing bludgeons. Where the green branches touched down and exploded, blasting the ground like rip-roaring TNT, a life form materialized out of thin air.

Suction.

Black Bat.

Centipede.

Crab.

They were worthy partners in war. Fireball raised up its head in pride and honor and welcomed them with another ear-piercing shriek. The monsters formed a semi-circle around Fireball and awaited new commands.

The ground below them kept shifting.

New rifts in the earth kept forming. Sinkholes widened and deepened. The ground used to be flat. Now there were hills, drops, and plateaus in the ice.

The battleground was set.

Any moment, Mega Mastodon would answer the call to protect the Earth from ultimate evil.

THEY'RE COMING

"I see them," Ted cried out in shock. "They're coming in all directions. Everybody stay low and out of sight. Be quiet. Maybe they'll walk right past us."

The group hid behind the bar. The sound of many feet crunching against snow could be heard. The constant echo of fire eating into buildings, cars, and the streets repeated. The sound was like air whooshing at high pressures. The people made no noises or spoke. They were drones of spitting fire.

There was a moment when their advancing was the loudest. Monica could tell the fire zombies were outside the windows at the apartment. Everybody held their breaths and prayed for safety.

Don't come inside. Nobody's here. Move on. Go away.

Please.

Just.

Go.

Away.

Fire ate into the neighboring buildings. The steady crackle became the night's soundtrack. Firelight glowed from the front entrance. Monica believed they would move on.

The wishful thinking earned her a great heap of disappointment.

The barricade at the stairs was suddenly bathed in flames from dozens of sources. The fire zombies plowed into the flaming debris, unafraid of burning. Shoving, kicking, and battering through the walls of fire and even catching themselves aflame in the process, the unbelievable enemies were hungry for inflicting death.

"The barricades didn't work," Ted growled. "Shit. Shit. Shit."

Smoke was filtering through the door. They would suffocate if they stayed in the strip club. Visibility was diminishing. Monica coughed against the choking smoke.

Deb cried out, "They're so horrible! This can't be real."

Human hands and faces were pressed against the glass. Fists punched the glass. Webs and forks spread against the pressure of their blows. Faces were peeled off and stuck to the glass when they head-butted the thin barrier. Bleeding, bare skulls were firing flames out of their eyes, noses, and mouths. The macabre sight got them moving fast.

Ted led the way up the stairs to the apartment buildings. Chip had a 12 gauge in tow. Monica only had the pickaxe, and Deb lugged a wooden baseball from behind the bar. The professor staggered, coming in last. He couldn't peel his gaze from the fire zombies.

Monica grabbed his arm. "Move it. There's no time to stare at them. They'll kill us all. We have to find a way out of this building before we all burn."

The glass door leading into the first floor of the apartments was already shattered. Fire zombies swarmed inside. Ted unloaded a clip of M-16 fire. The bullets chewed through their bodies and knocked them back long enough for them to lunge up the next flight of stairs.

"Try one of the apartments," Chip yelled, giving them more time to maneuver by shooting three times with his twelve gauge. "There has to be a fire exit."

Screams rang out from inside the apartments. The few who had hidden in their homes were being attacked. Monica could hear the fire zombies climb the emergency stairs on the outside of the building. Fire was eating up the walls. Smoke was pouring in all directions.

Ted reloaded a magazine into the machine gun. "Last clip, folks."

Chip lost his footing and tripped down the stairs, rolling right into a wall of fire zombies. The group of roasting-fleshed, fire-eyed enemies doused him in orange. Monica cried out in horror as Chip's flesh was instantly incinerated down to the bone.

"Chip! *Noooooo!*"

Ted didn't hesitate to open fire. Most of the shots went wild. Whenever more than two or three bullets penetrated a body, the whole torso collapsed from their middle and an eruption of flames burst from their fire-ridden bodies.

"We only have to hold them off for so long," the professor shouted. "The fire is burning them up from the inside. Their bodies can't take much any longer."

"Neither can we," Ted growled. "I'm out of ammo."

The apartment doors all around Deb burst open. Burner jets of flames coated her flailing body. So hot, her flesh bubbled and boiled and became so soft and hot, it was like her skin was wax. The cooking flesh slapped the walls and slid down her bones in disgusting consistencies. The rest of Deb's body soon struck the floor dead.

The professor charged the incoming fire zombies. He pushed and shoved even as they were spitting fire at his body. Half of him was ablaze.

"Run! Save yourselves. I'm ready to see my wife and son again. NOW GET OUT OF HERE!"

The professor's wails of being cooked alive propelled them up the final flight of stairs to the third floor. The roof's exit was the final stop. Smoke and flames blurred the scene. She could barely see Ted. When her sight cleared enough to see what he was doing, she gasped.

He had two grenades clutched in his hands. "I've been saving these for years. I mail ordered them. I could never use them. You can fire a gun at a target range, but you sure can't test these babies out. I've lost everything tonight, Monica. My family. My friends. Everything has been burned to nothing. You get up on that roof and find a way to survive this. I'll buy you time. I wish you well, Monica. I haven't known you long, but I know you're a good kid. Now go live your life. Don't let our deaths be for nothing."

He pushed her through the roof exit. Ted slammed the door shut and locked her out. She could hear him counting down from five.

"Five...four...three...two...ONE!"

The grenades did the job.

Monica ducked to avoid the door when it was blown from its hinges. Flames were shooting out of the door. Smoke from many sources was billowing from the exit/entry. Nothing moved for minutes. And then the other half of the fire zombies made their way up the stairs.

They were coming right for her.

CLOSE CALL

The apartment building below her was a raging inferno. She could hear fire eating up every panel inch of the structure. The tar on top of the roof was beginning to smoke and bubble. Things were getting hot. The temperature seconded the approaching people shambling through the door. Their movements weren't as fast before. They were walking briquettes of charcoal. Any kiss of wind turned them into the tips of cigarettes being pulled by nicotine-hungry lips. Some fire zombies stepped onto the roof for their legs to crumble into brisket falling off the bones. Others simply burst into great flames, their combustible bodies going up. Still, there were some who were still coming nearer with arms outstretched and eyes spewing flames.

Monica gasped when the backs of her feet hit the roof's edge. She had almost buckled over backwards and fell off the three-story building.

Should she jump?

The only way out was through the fire zombies, and even worse, a furnace of flames. The equation added up to death. How much agony could she take?

Should I jump? she kept thinking.

She thought about her life again. How things went from bad to worse, then to awesome, and then finally to this madness…

"Duck for cover!"

The approaching fire zombies were shredded by hard-hitting machine gun fire. Walls of bullets hammered home the message of death. Burning hot chunks of bodies splattered the roof as bullets disembodied piping hot bodies.

Up above, a military chopper lowered a rope ladder.

Monica didn't hesitate to climb to safety.

A man with a flat-top hair cut in a black-and-gray camouflage uniform helped her up. He was the one who manned the turret machine gun on the side of the chopper. She could still smell the smoke and feel the heating coming off those long, blued barrels.

Fire zombies continued to file out of the roof's entry and burn. It was easy to gather she would either be dead or cooked crispy if it weren't for these people.

"Thank you for saving my life. That was close."

"Just doing my job, ma'am." The man saluted her. "I'm Sergeant Chambers. Pleased to meet you. Sorry it has to be under such poor circumstances."

There were two others in the helicopter. The pilot who said nothing and a scientist-looking guy who was a younger and geekier version of the professor.

That geek turned to greet her. "I'm Brian McCullough. Director of the Geological Survey."

"What does that mean?"

"It means whenever something fucked up comes out of the ground, the government hires me to study it and identify it."

"So what is that flying thing that's killing everybody?"

"You mean Fireball?"

"No. I mean the other flying asshole in the sky. Yes, Fireball!" Monica didn't mean to snap. "Look, I'm sorry. I've had a long day."

"Me too," Brian said. "No need to apologize. I've lost people I've loved throughout the day. I'm sure you have too."

"Do you know about the mastodons?"

"The mastodons? No."

She explained the electrical surge that brought back the cavemen and the mastodons. She went on about the Professor Sterling's dig site, and how he was on the verge of finding new prehistoric creatures.

"I have to see them."

"No can do. Fireball destroyed them all. There's nothing left."

Brian had a big black box with a computerized screen. The box gave a sharp beeping noise. "More shifting of the earth hundreds of feet under the ground. Something's trying to make its way to the surface. And whatever it is, it's huge."

Sergeant Chambers was getting a message on his headset. "Fireball is staying in that general area. Whatever's under that ice, it's the reason he's stayed here so long. If that damn thing would stay in one place for more than ten minutes before vanishing and transporting itself elsewhere, we can annihilate it."

"Nuclear weapons didn't work," Brian countered. "It only made him stronger. Our ballistics tests proved its armor can withstand bullets, missiles, fire, and whatever else you have to throw at it."

"We haven't tried everything just yet." Chambers' face twisted into a maniacal grin. "The Commander-in-Chief has given us every tool in the catalogue to fight this thing. Even the untested weapons. I've worked with a lot of different people who've created a lot of interesting weaponry. We're going to have some serious fireworks in the coming minutes. We've got a lot of crazy shit the Army would never use on the battlefield…except for tonight. I'm extinguishing Fireball for good."

"Wait a second," Monica said. "This helicopter is going into battle?"

"You betcha," Chambers said. "We need every set of hands. You're going to join in on the fun."

"She'll stay with me, Sergeant," Brian said. "I want to see that dig site. I have an idea. We're desperate, aren't we? We have to try everything."

Brian turned to Monica. An apology showed in his eyes. "I wish this was a rescue mission where we got to go home. The war isn't over. We don't win this one, there'll be no home to go to. I need your help. Can I count on you? Will you show me the dig site?"

"I won't allow it," Chambers said. "You're coming onto the battlefield with us. Everybody's necks are in the noose together. You're no exception."

"I was told I can investigate Fireball to the fullest extent. That's what I intend to do. You have the president backing you up. That same president is backing me up. Braun won't win the battle. Brains will.

"We're having all kinds of activity under the ground where Fireball has stayed for more than two hours. Every other place he's attacked, he made an appearance for ten, maybe fifteen minutes. This means something. Whatever's under the ground is important. I have to know what it is. It could help us."

"Can't let you go. I don't have the men."

"Monica and I will go together. I'll stay in constant contact. I won't take any of your men."

"I said no. I've been left in charge of your safety. You're not going anywhere."

Brian was fuming. "All you care about is getting to use your banned weapons. You want to turn this into a commercial to sell new weaponry and technologies? Hey. Great. Super duper. I'm not stopping you. Point and shoot all you want. I'm only asking for the right to do a proper investigation. It could save our lives. You still care about human life, don't you, Sergeant?"

"I care about getting the job done, and that's what I'm going to do. I'm not going to be challenged by a tiny insect like you. You sit down and shut up before I do something you'll regret making me do. Discussion time is over."

Monica couldn't believe what Brian did next.

It would change the course of everything.

PART FOUR: EPIC BATTLE

HARD CHOICES

"Put the gun down!"

Brian had a 9mm pressed against the pilot's head. "I will not, Sergeant. Now where is this dig site, Monica?"

Monica told them it wasn't far from where Fireball was currently located. The site was on the edge of a wide-open area where Fireball kept showering the ground with ball after ball of fire.

"Okay," Brian instructed. "Put this whirly bird down. Monica and I are going on a little expedition. Got a problem with that?"

"Yes, I do!" Chambers wanted to reach out and strangle Brian. "This isn't the time to dig in the dirt."

"I don't care, sir."

"We're here," Monica said. "Straight below us. I can show you. It won't take long."

Chambers snarled. "Fine. If you're going down, we're leaving you. Anything attacks you, any friendly fire goes in your direction, there's nothing I can do. Your life is yours to lose. I cannot protect you if you disobey my rules."

"I've considered your position, and I'm not changing mine. Drop this thing to the ground."

"You're making a huge mistake. You might as well be dead. Our country needs you here with me. Not out there digging around in the dirt."

"I know what my country needs," Brian said. "Our country needs you, *asshole*, to get off my back and let me do my job. I'll blow our pilot's head off, and we'll all crash and burn if you don't do as I say."

Chambers scoffed. "You won't hurt anybody. But I don't want cowards beside me when the shit gets thick and steaming. Put down your gun, idiot. I'll drop you off. And when this is over, I'll have you tried to treason."

RETRACING STEPS

Brian helped Monica out of the helicopter when it touched down near the dig site. Right before the chopper lifted back off, Chambers yelled down at them.

"You'll be sorry! By the end of this, you'll be executed on live TV."

"Chambers," Brian yelled back. "I am sick of you. You've been riding me the moment we met. Go eat out of a colostomy bag!"

Chambers' eyes flared in anger. Then he indicated to the pilot to take off. Once they were left alone, the scene grew intensely quiet. The area was pitch black. Brian dug into his backpack to retrieve his flashlight. He shined it on the dig site.

"*Wow*," Brian gasped. "What came out of the ground?"

The entrance to the dig sight looked to have exploded. Mastodon tracks were pounded into the snow. A police car had been squashed by their exit. She could still see where the officers on the scene were killed by the red staining the snow.

Monica described the cavemen and the mastodons. She went on about Professor Sterling's findings.

"Scientific journals have been buzzing about this place for awhile," Brian said. "And you're telling me these things were alive?"

"Alive and killing. The cavemen terrorized the town and murdered just about everybody. Then that thing in the sky, it turned people—"

"Into killing machines?"

"Yes."

"It's happened in several cities. Wherever that thing takes a leak, people are contaminated. It turns them into human torches.

Eventually, they burn out. It takes about a couple of hours, weather depending. It might've taken longer here because it's below freezing outside. The hotter cities, they were dead within twenty minutes."

"You really want to see down there in the hole?" Monica pointed to what looked like the entry into the below ground site. "We might not be able to get down. You see, there was an electrical surge that brought those cavemen back to life. I'm not sure if there's any more of them down there. It's something out of a Frankenstein movie. I wouldn't believe it if I hadn't seen it."

"I believe you," Brian insisted. "I'm very interested in this sight. Fireball's attacks are quick and devastating. Here, he's stuck around, and he's hovering several miles from here. Something is keeping him here. What is it?"

She could see the rings of fire burn in the distance. Fireball shrieked every now and again from up in the sky.

Brian was right.

Something had the creature worked up.

"He's waiting for something in the ground, we know that," Brian offered. "There's movement from something huge under the ground. Any moment, it'll break free."

"What do you think it is?

"No idea. My guess…a natural enemy of Fireball. Professor Sterling's theories about the earth shifting millions of years ago and dumping life forms from across the world to this very spot could be accurate. If you say there was an electrical surge that brought back those cavemen and those mastodons, I'm very curious about what else it might've brought back to life."

"Then let's go. I'll lead the way."

The wooden scaffolding leading to the bottom had seen better days. Some of the mastodons had treaded hard enough to split boards and punch through them completely. The structure's integrity was in question. She voiced this concern. Brian didn't care. He was determined to find out what was alive under the ground.

After descending and taking care not to fall, they arrived at the bottom. The earth was torn and twisted up. Where the caveman scene had been before everything happened, a giant hole had formed. She imagined great hands pushing up underneath to break free.

"This is simply amazing," Brian said. "This is a real piece of history. I have nothing but fond respect for Randall Sterling. He was onto something great."

"He died fighting," Monica said. "He deserves full credit for whatever good comes out of this horror."

"Absolutely."

Brian's awe soured into disgust. He caught sight of a pile of mutilated body parts and partially eaten corpses. "Oh God. What is that from?"

"The cavemen. They're cannibals. They killed Randall's son and many people in town. They were savages."

"Sickening."

They stopped at the giant gaping hole where the mastodons had escaped. Brian gave her a sideways smile. "Care to see what's down below?"

"I've been through so much already. I'm not afraid of anything anymore. Okay. Let's go."

EMPTY RECESS

The ground was rock hard. Ice surrounded the overhanging walls where the mastodons had somehow pounded their way free. Monica could see where electrical currents had broken up the walls and opened up recesses that were otherwise frozen solid. Ancient history had been buried here and preserved. It would've been amazing if it hadn't led to so many people being dead.

The two kept treading forward. The tunnel went on and on. The way got colder. The caliber of cold that penetrated bone. She could freeze to death in this climate. She talked to get her mind off of the chill.

"Where did Fireball come from?"

"Basically Hawaii. A dormant volcano became active unexpectedly. Lava covered the island, and Fireball must've been sleeping under that lava. God knows how it survived. The thing is living fire. It has attacked places all across the world. The government wanted to study it, at first. Now they just want to kill it.

"Fireball only grew stronger when they deployed a nuclear missile. The monster simply swallowed it up. The power from the bomb gave it new abilities. I swear this is a freakin' science fiction novel. It can teleport itself from place to place in a blink. It also summoned up new friends from deep in the earth. They disappeared for a time, but now they're back, and they're here, Monica. A big battle is underway. It's happening here, I'm convinced.

"We have to learn as much as we can before Sergeant Chambers does something that can kill whoever is left alive in this area. My greater fear...if he uses another weapon like a nuke, that monster could absorb its energy and simply grow more powerful. Anything can happen. That's what I'm scared of."

She couldn't believe what she was hearing. "Everything's happening so fast. I haven't heard much about what the rest of the world has gone through. When Fireball broke free, I think that's around when those cavemen came to life."

"Fireball's been reaping havoc for barely twenty-four hours. The beast moves fast. It's all coming together full circle. This is the ultimate battle for the world. Humanity may lose this one."

The thought was as dire and hopeless as the walls were blue with ice.

"Hold on. What is this?"

Brian moved ahead of her. There were trenches cut in the ice. Holes were punched in the walls. They felt a breeze cross them. Hurrying on, they could see the night sky.

Whatever was under the ground was now free.

They could hear the sounds of war breaking out on the surface.

The ultimate battle had indeed begun.

TAKE COMMAND

Brian McCullough could go fuck himself, Sergeant Chambers thought, gritting his teeth in anger. The egghead could feed Greek salads, formulas, and equations into a machine and only get things published in textbooks. The sergeant had greater aspirations than publication. The military had been pushing for better funding for new weapons technologies. This went beyond nuclear missiles. These weapons would make their enemies piss their pants. Terrorists would think twice before sending off their suicide bombers to kill innocent people. This unreal situation was the perfect arena to encourage new and experimental awesome weaponry. By the end of this, the American public would pay any amount of taxes for protection.

The main thing was the main thing, he thought. Kill Fireball. Destroy Fireball's friends. Save the world. Then plunge his hands deeply into America's piggy bank and get insanely rich. Sergeant Chambers had a wide selection of investors and weapons companies who would use him as a figure to spearhead these lucrative products into the future.

The main thing is the main thing, he repeated mentally. *Let's kick some ass.*

The chopper touched down on the edge of what the sergeant considered the battlefield. That battlefield was marked by flames burning the ground. Fireball kept hovering in the air, circling the same spot. The other towering monsters stayed in position as sentries awaiting command from their leader.

A tent was set up as temporary base on the outskirts of the battlefield. Cargo planes were bringing in troops and special weaponry. Things were coming into motion quickly. The Commander-in-Chief gave Chambers a one hundred percent green light to take out the target. He would take full advantage of that go-ahead and really do some damage.

The cargo planes finally landed one by one and unloaded special weapons from every post. Troops were positioned just outside the imaginary square of the battlefield in all cardinal directions.

"Those monsters sure are ugly," Sergeant Guyer commented, greeting Chambers in the giant tent that did little to block out the cold. A table was set up. A map of the battlefield was drawn. Both of them studied it closely. "I can't wait to splatter their guts against the snow. We'll obliterate them all. They'll be dead monster meat."

"I can't wait to see them go down too," the sergeant agreed. "We have a crew recording the process. I hired them out of my own pocket. We can use that video as a demo to fund new weapons production. Marketing will be easy when our weapons crush the most dangerous targets in human history."

"We'll be stinking rich," Guyer said, high-fiving his long-time friend and counterpart in military service. "We'll take off our fatigues and put on business suits. We'll sell this shit and make a killing. America will be so scared after what they've seen, tax money will pour in like crazy."

"Fish in a barrel," the sergeant laughed. "Or should I say…Fireball in a barrel? *Hah-hah-hah.* The president promised us many things if we pull off this mission. This'll be the biggest free enterprise opportunity. America's economy will be bolstered by weapons technologies."

The sergeant had communication from the frontlines.

The special weapons were ready to be unleashed on the enemy.

MOLECULAR DISPLACER

Bernie Price awaited word from Sergeant Chambers for the go-ahead attack. Price wasn't military personal. He was a weapons engineer by trade. They were working hand-in-hand with the military personnel on site to make this defensive front a successful one.

Soldiers surrounded Price and two of his assistants while unloading the Molecular Displacer Cannon from the cargo airship. They were approximately a mile from the field of battle. He still couldn't believe his eyes. Fireball towered in the sky, unleashing fireball after fireball upon the earth. Fire was in endless supply for this being, he thought. The monsters weren't distracted by their presence. Something else was keeping them busy.

I'm fine with that.

That gives us more time to unload a can of whoop ass.

The molecular displacer was a giant black cannon. Atomic energy met with science to make this very experimental weapon a reality. One direct hit from this baby could rearrange a victim on a cellular level. It could displace organs about the body, causing guaranteed death.

"*Let 'er rip, Mr. Price,*" the sergeant said over the walkie. "*Kill shots only. One hundred percent destruction. I want this thing's head blasted out of its monster ass. That's what you promised.*"

"You got it, Sergeant," Price relayed. "Sign, sealed, and delivered. I promise mission success. Just sit back and watch. Go ahead and pour that celebratory glass of whiskey."

Price and his two assistants were plugging in coordinates.

"Who are you going to kill first?" Boatwright, Price's assistant, asked. "They're all pretty nasty."

Price smiled at his long time buddy. "That bat bugs the shit out of me. Its beady red eyes. I bet it has rabies, malaria, and probably something that makes your pecker ooze slime. I'm going to make that bastard even more ugly before I destroy it."

The electrical board on the side of the cannon was lit up with reds, blues, and green lights. The cannon buzzed with energy. The molecular displacer was ready to do its job.

"Cannon fully charged and ready," Boatwright announced. "Ready to hit the switch when you are, boss."

Price checked his panels. The molecular displacer was ready to do what its name promised. Displace monster ass.

"Ready to hit the switch on…four…three…two…ONE!"

Black Bat sensed the attack. Its overlarge sensitive ears twitched. The bat rose up, flying headfirst to answer the call of defense.

Price's eyes were bulbous and insane watching the cannon fire. A giant crackle of atomic energy burst from the cannon. A beam of blue light crackling with white energy particles a quarter mile long was hurled right into the bat's direction.

"Suck on that, bat bitch!" Price howled. "You're fucking dead!"

The neon blue beam struck the bat in the chest. The bat unleashed a piercing cry as it was thrown backwards. Before its lungs could send out that high-pitched cry that could pop heads, its anatomy changed. Its flesh was flipped inside out. The bat was pink skinned and spurting red from broken bodily processes. Its heart pumped at its throat. The head was now in its chest cavity. The wings were where its legs normally would be. Two legs protruded from its head. The twitching, writhing mass of agony crashed down onto the ice. It flailed and spurted blood for ten long seconds before the creature finally died.

"Yes!" Price high-fived everybody. "That kicked ass. You see that beam sear into its body? Rearranged that flying piece of shit real quick. Take that!"

The soldiers broke their stoic concentration to smile and enjoy the victorious moment. Everybody was delighted by the results.

"Kicked your ass," Boatwright kept repeating. "Kicked your ass. Yeah. Kicked your stupid bat ass."

The molecular displacer was heating up. Smoke poured from the machine. Price and Boatwright punched buttons, frantically trying to cool it off.

"It's overloaded!"

"There's something wrong."

"I thought this was one hundred percent functional."

"We've barely tested it."

"It's going to blow!"

"Oh shit! Run!"

The molecular displacer burst, shedding blue light and hunks of shrapnel metal. That light penetrated everybody in its near proximity. Soldiers hit the snow, turned inside out, their organs and limbs mismatched about their bodies. The macabre sight was horrible to take in. Price would've lost his mind if it wasn't for the excruciating pain of having his head where his right arm should be. His heart was in one hand, and his testicles were in the other.

Everybody on sight died in true agony.

"You see that bat go down?" Stapleton was cheering. "That was beautiful."

Guyer was hung up on the blue explosion. "But all those people are dead. Jesus, it's horrible. Some of them are still screaming in pain."

"A few drops of blood in the name of progress isn't too much to ask." The sergeant called out to the rest of the units. "EVERYBODY FIRE AT WILL! I WANT THEM ALL DEAD!"

ALL OUT WAR

Terry "The Tank" Newman was driving a hybrid vehicle. Imagine a tank merged with a Hummer. The wheels were changed out to drive on snow and ice. On top of the roof were five rockets ready to fire. These were very special rockets. He liked to brag he was driving two billion dollars on wheels. He jumped at the chance to use his vehicle in defending America from this menace.

"Up your ass and into the grave, you ugly motherfuckers," he muttered, driving up to the edge of the battlefield. "When you wipe your ass, all you'll get is blood."

He heard the call to unleash all firepower from the sergeant. The Black Bat had gone down, eliminating one target. The Tank noticed one thing that troubled him. The monsters acted oblivious to their presence up to moments ago. Now all four monsters were ready to take them on. Was this the monster's strategy? Give them false confidence?

They had to die, he thought. They were way too smart for monsters.

The giant pale gray crab was on all fours and crunching through the snow at eighty miles an hour. Those pincers had torn buildings in half and killed hundreds of thousands of innocent people. Suction, the enormous Manta Ray-like enemy, with ten giant mouths on its belly, was up in the air spinning in place, gaining suction power by the second. Centipede was pounding thousands of legs on the ground and coming at them in a slithery motion. And the most powerful creature, Fireball himself, was up in the sky overseeing the charge.

"You're in for some bad weather," The Tank growled. "The forecast calls for YOUR ASS!"

The Tank deployed all five rockets on the top of the vehicle.

Soooooooooooooonk!
Soooooooooooooonk!
Soooooooooooooonk!
Soooooooooooooonk!
Soooooooooooooonk!

The rockets exploded over and under the collection of incoming enemies. Each explosion mingled together, creating a literal funnel cloud of wind. The wind grew faster and faster, spinning as a tornado times ten.

The beasts were sucked right into the funnel. Even Fireball was flipped upside down and struggling to regain its bearings.

"You're nothing but trash trapped in my funnel. Soon, I'll hear your bones breaking one by one. The force will destroy you from the inside out. Once the cloud ends, it'll rain your meat."

The swirling cloud of force kept spinning and thrashing them around. They were objects in a high-speed blender, helpless to the cyclonic force. The Tank was counting the dollars he would make off of saving the world's ass. And just how much ass would he pull for being a real life superhero? Forget Superman. The Tank was the real deal. He would be written into history books as the biggest ass kicker ever. He imagined talk shows and maybe a movie deal. *The Tank: Story of A True American Hero.* The title might need work. The message was there. The Tank's weaponry was first class in taking out monster trash.

Everything was going as planned until a voice on the radio spoke to him.

It was Craig Fuller.

Craig was pissed.

"I don't think so, Tank. You're not taking all the credit. I worked just as hard as you to get to this point. You showed off your toy. Now it's time to show off mine."

"You idiot! You do anything to change the funnel cloud, you'll ruin everything. I'll share the credit. Give the funnel another five minutes. When the cycle is over, you'll have your fair shot. Craig, you have to hear me out! For God's sake, DON'T!"

"Fuck you, Tank. Watch me in action!"

Tank knew it before anything happened.

This mission was doomed.

SPECTACLE

Craig Fuller was standing on a raised steel platform. All around him stood cannons. Fifty total. They each harbored different rockets. Some would unleash flames that could rival Fireball's. Others had nuclear capabilities. Others could displace air and use pressure to squash a target. Others used sonar waves to break up land into pieces and make an enemy's progress fall flat. All he had to do was press one button and end the battle.

His crew of twelve assistants was quickly checking that the rockets were aimed at the correct target. The Tank had done him one favor. He had brought all the targets together in that single funnel cloud.

"This one's for you, Sergeant," Fuller said, after getting the go-ahead from his team. "BLAST 'EM!"

Fifty rockets thundered off at once, each one zooming straight for the funnel cloud.

"*Ye-aaaaaaaaah!*" Fuller pumped his fist in the air. "WATCH IT RAIN BLOOD!"

The funnel was increasing in speed. The monsters were twisted up in the invisible force of air. Infernal shrieks and cries of helpless monsters were pleasing to his ears.

"Sir," one of Fuller's lackeys flagged his attention. She had horror in her eyes. "Our missiles can't lock onto the target. The speed of that funnel is throwing everything off. The missiles won't hit their target."

"What do you mean they won't hit their targets?"

Fuller didn't get an answer to his question. He could see it happen up there in the sky for himself. Each rocket was heading for the cloud. Once they were within a certain range, the missiles veered off in all directions. Most of the rockets went hurling into the nearby towns, blowing up cities. Others were headed right back to their source.

"*Noooooooooooo!*"

Fuller and his crew were instantly disintegrated.

DEPLOY THE TROOPS

"Of all the fuck ups that could happen," Sergeant Chambers growled. "Damn it all! Okay. Plan B. Deploy the troops. They've been trained to use their special guns. This is our last chance. We cannot fuck this up."

"What if they can't stop them?" Guyer asked. "Then what?"

"Then we're fucked. We lost most of our defense fighting Fireball earlier. This is it. We can't win this fight, well, we've…we'll go down in defeat. I hate to say it. But that's the truth."

Cargo planes had delivered nearly five thousand troops. They were waiting inside the planes to go on the attack, if necessary. The sergeant addressed them all at once on a radio frequency.

"Okay, boys. Sounds like Plan A blew up in our faces. You have the weaponry to take them down. You've been instructed on how to use your special guns. Show off your training, boys. You win this battle, booze and hookers are on me! NOW GO KICK SOME ASS!"

The sergeant exited the tent. He watched the troops storm out of the back of the cargo aircraft in mass numbers. He was proud of their fearlessness.

For the first time during this Alaskan battle, he was worried.

They could lose this battle.

The coming moments would mean the world.

The funnel cloud ebbed back into calm air. The monsters were dizzy and landed awkwardly against the ground. The group sensed foot soldiers coming for them. Green flashing beams burst from thousands of discharging laser guns. Fireball took the first few hits. They singed his scales, sending deliveries of pain deep into his nerve centers. The other monsters also took hits from laser guns. Their growls of pain turned into battle cries.

Fireball again led the charge.

Blood would soon follow.

Officer Brewer was among the five thousand soldiers charging the beasts. He didn't lie. He was scared shitless. The laser gun in his clutches was shaped like a Carbine rifle. The lasers were concentrated beams of light that could penetrate through the thickest of steel…and the hope, scales, plates, and crab shell.

Brewer unloaded laser blast after laser blast. The whole thing was a shit show, he realized. They were buying time. Maybe Sergeant Stapleton had another plan that required stalling the monsters even longer. Perhaps the sergeant had his head up his ass and was already retreating the area to save his own skin.

The giant dark brown centipede was fast and sleek moving. It sucked up soldiers like the brush of a street sweeper. Each person sucked in didn't come back. Not a drop of blood spattered anywhere. They were simply…devoured.

Brewer dropped to the ground for cover. Out reached a giant crab hand. The pincer closed around two hundred soldiers and squeezed. The sound of pain as two hundred sets of legs were separated from torsos was insane to overhear. When Brewer got up, he was treading through steaming hot intestines and organs.

He kept firing his laser gun at the monsters. When his gun ran out, he pried another from a dead soldier's grasp. There were plenty to choose from.

The determined soldier hit the ground again. He sensed the pull of air from above that he was warned about. Dubbed "Suction" by the media, the giant manta ray-like creature was spinning in the air like a top. Brewer's eyes bulged in their sockets watching flesh be wrenched from bodies and limbs torn from sockets from the air pressure's force.

Another thousand soldiers dropped dead against the ice. Rivers of blood flowed hot at his feet before turning ice cold. The soldiers that survived the immediate onslaught were scattered and frantically blasting their useless laser guns. The beams annoyed the beasts more than anything else.

They were promised the lasers would do serious damage to the enemy.

The sergeant's reassurance was either misguided or completely false.

The son-of-a-bitch put us in harm's way carelessly.

I hope Chambers is court marshaled and hanged.

That's if there's anybody left alive to do so.

The facts and miscalculations wouldn't matter. Fireball towered over the battlefield littered with battered body parts and ribbons of flesh. The dragon beast opened its deadly mouth and bathed them in a shower of unholy fire. The fires scorched every trace of military presence. Even the sergeant's tent was burned so fast, those inside were instantly cooked to bare bones.

Silence fell on the battlefield.

Nothing remained in the way of Fireball's plan of world destruction and domination.

Almost nothing.

THE TANK

The Tank was smart by driving away from the battlefield. The soldiers deployed were being slaughtered. He literally saw human limbs fly up into the air as high as skyscraper buildings. Fires burned the rest of the fighters. The stench of cooked flesh could be sensed all the way from his safe vantage point. "Safe" being a relative word.

He damned Fuller for ruining what would've killed those monsters. A little longer in the funnel would've broken the monsters' bones and stopped them for good.

It's too late for would've, should've, could've. No cry babies here. Only tough, barbed-wire chewing sons-of-bitches reporting for duty.

Sergeant Chambers wasn't answering his frequency. The man was dead too. He was on his own.

I'm the only man left alive, he thought. *They don't call me The Tank for nothing. I'm down, but I'm not out. I'm not completely dry of ammo. I was smart enough to come with reloads.*

The reloads were strapped to the bottom of his vehicle in a special holding area. It would take him a good twenty minutes to sneak under the truck, carry each rocket, put them into the cannon, and return to the truck to fire them.

He prayed he couldn't be seen from so far away by the monsters.

All he needed was one distraction.

Give him twenty minutes, he kept thinking, and he could take back America.

Up from the earth, that seventy-ton distraction finally made its appearance.

BREAKING THE ICE

Mega Mastodon had tunneled upwards for hours and hours. The frozen earth grew easier to pummel with its front feet and hammer at with its giant tusks. The prehistoric beast could sense its enemy topside. Fireball had already eaten and killed its children that had escaped hours ago. The cries of this father's children being mercilessly stalked and slaughtered drew rancor in this already pissed off animal.

Carving and tunneling upwards with another great surge, the mastodon, easily ten times the size of an average mastodon, rose up from the earth to face its enemies. Every instinct told this father if any of its children or fellow race were still alive, Fireball would consume them all. This beast of the ice couldn't allow Fireball to live.

Ice and earth exploded from the ground. Launching up from the earth as if spring ejected, the mastodon landed on what used to be the human battlefield.

Now it was beast battleground.

Mega Mastodon huffed, lifted itself up on its hind legs, and unleashed a battle cry roar. Out its trunk, whistles of angry air grew louder. The noises were a come on for battle.

Fireball, turning around having just roasted what was left of the soldiers, met the stare of its sworn enemy through time. Millions of years ago, Fireball enjoyed raiding homes and hideaways of mastodons and eating their children. Sometimes, while the baby was half-way out of the mother's womb, the dragon would snatch it up by the legs and steal the baby before the newborn's eyes had seen the light of day. The succulent, tender meat of baby mastodons still to this day drew saliva from its mouth. And now it was hungry for adult mastodon meat.

Mega Mastodon charged forward, rampaging at fifty miles an hour to take on the collection of beasts by himself.

Carnage would ensue.

WATCHING THE SHOW

Monica crawled out of the gaping hole Mega Mastodon had created when it escaped. She stood topside with Brian. They were both scanning the horizon in awe. Signs of military presence didn't serve to reassure them. Broken and charred bodies were scattered everywhere. They did nothing to stop the monster threat.

"Chambers didn't think this through," Brian sighed. "The monsters were too powerful for his special weaponry. You have to outsmart the beast. In this case…we may have to let nature take its course. I know our country is hurrying to stop this threat, but sometimes you have to take a minute and really see what's happening."

"How can anyone human fix this problem? No one's truly equipped." Monica was getting tired of conjecture. "And what if one huge mastodon can't kill four creatures of equal size? It's not exactly a fair fight."

"Well, one thing is for certain. That mastodon is pissed."

"So what do we do now besides shiver in the cold?"

Brian checked every channel of the short wave radio. He called for any survivors. He grumbled with every passing second. "Nobody's out there. We'll have to take it on foot back to the city."

"Yeah, but those things'll see us."

"It's a chance we have to take. We'll freeze to death staying out here."

They both looked towards the field of battle. Monica and Brian were instantly entranced. Mega Mastodon used its massively powerful legs to vault upwards. It landed down, stomping all four into the hindquarters of Centipede. One quarter of its body squished under the powerful force. Yellow guts squirted from cracks in its plating. Using its enormous tusks, it flipped the centipede off of the ground and hurled it off the battlefield.

Suction was above the mastodon warrior and about to unleash a powerful suck in retaliation. Mega Mastodon answered the threat. Craning its neck up at the sky, its mega tusks acted as missiles and fired upwards. One tusk missed. The other pierced the left side of Suction's body. The tusk cut through one flap and out the other side. Black blood drizzled down, covering the snow in inky puddles the size of small lakes. Suction spun out, landing so hard, it rolled across the ice and stayed where it lay for moments before trying to muster the strength for another attack.

New tusks were produced from the empty slots. Reloaded, Mega Mastodon raged on. Crab met its advances. Pincers were clacking and reaching, trying to give the mastodon the squeeze. Each clack was a concussion to the ground. Monica and Brian had to stay hunched on the ground or else get knocked down.

The mastodon weaved like a star running back going in for the touchdown from halfway down the field. The hairy beast was goading Crab. The mastodon stopped suddenly and let the pursuing Crab crash into him head first. Head to head, the mastodon's extra thick skull gave extra force to the blow. Crab's left black beady eye popped like a grape. Half of its face was oozing bright green blood. From mastodon's fleshy trunk, it sneezed. Out spewed a sticky mucous concoction that covered Crab from top to bottom. The stuff was so sticky and hardened so fast, Crab was stuck like a fly in an intricate spider's web.

Mega Mastodon threw backs its trunk and unleashed a high-pitched song. It glared at Fireball with eyes seething rage. Fireball replied by releasing five fireballs in its direction. The mastodon bounced back and forth, avoiding the short concourse of flames.

Fireball swooped down. From its outspread wings, jets of flames doused the terrain. Everything was over bright. Mega Mastodon leaped up, lunging right for Fireball's torso. The beast grazed Fireball's plate with its tusk. Scales were ripped from its body. The surface gash was a hundred feet long. The front half of Mega Mastodon was busy with flames. It rolled its massive body against the snow, putting out the flames before doing any serious damage.

Both beasts were posed across from each other again.

And once again, both monsters ran at the other to strike another blow.

Eventually, one would be a killing blow.

A CHANCE IN HELL

Monica watched the beginning of the showdown. They were enamored with each monster's moves. Fireball had batted the mastodon with its wing, throwing it across the ice. The struck beast got right back up and fired another tusk from long range. It pierced right through Fireball's left wing, creating a large gaping hole in the leathery fabric. Both were charging head to head yet again.

The piercing headlights in the snow stole their attention.

"What the hell is that?" Brian asked. "It looks like a SUV combined with a tank."

She was too busy checking out the shark teeth decal along both its doors.

The vehicle parked in front of them. Monica couldn't see much of the man through his thermal gear and goggles. He had a thick bushy beard and a voice that sounded like a burned-out roadie for an '80's hair band.

"You survived this long. Rock on. People call me The Tank. I need your help. I can end this mess if you care to assist me."

"Of course," Monica said. "Anything."

"Yeah," Brian added. "Whatever you need."

"I need to reload some rockets on my vehicle. I'll hand them to you. You put them into the device. It's that easy."

The Tank crawled underneath his vehicle. He talked over the roar of battle. "These rockets are pretty damn heavy. It'll take all three of us to load them. You're going to save me so much time."

"Who are you?" Monica asked. "I mean, where did you come from?"

"That'll take some explaining. The military is desperate. Most of our military forces were used up fighting Fireball throughout the day. We were America's last resort. I create weapons technologies for a private company. I used my weapons earlier. I had the suckers in my sight, and, you see, well, never mind. Forget it. We got one more shot, basically. Anyway, these rockets create a super tornado. It'll spin these monsters up high and break every bone in their body."

Monica struggled to take it all in. "This is all so unbelievable."

"Get used to unbelievable," The Tank said. "We got monsters coming out of volcanoes and out of the ground. Using your imagination to suspend disbelief helps. It's this simple. I'll reload my guns and take another shot at killing these things."

Monica and Brian helped Tank carry a single rocket from under the cargo space beneath the vehicle. They loaded it up on the roof top's steel box firing case.

There were four rockets more to go.

BATTLE SHIFT

Mega Mastodon delivered three powerful head-butts to Fireball's skull. Blood was oozing from its dragon nostrils in thick currents. Four teeth on top and three on bottom had been shattered. The dragon spit them out across the ice in rage. The mastodon had sustained damage as well. The right side of its body had been burned badly enough to reveal glistening meat. Its back leg was bleeding from a bite wound. Part of its knee bone and femur could be seen through the gnarly thick pink muscle tissue.

Still, the monsters did battle.

The one-on-one fight was about to end.

Crab had broken free from its mucous ropes and was clacking its way back into the fight. Centipede had flicked off the broken quarter of its body and used its own burning saliva juices to cauterize the wound. The plated bug weaved its way onwards, closing in on its enemy. Suction was airborne again, ready to suck flesh.

The beast was outnumbered. The odds were against him. The coming moments would prove crucial to the fate of the world.

Centipede crawled across the top of Mega Mastodon's back. Hundreds of belly mouths stole tiny rivulets of flesh. The mastodon unleashed a peal of pain as blood leaked down its back.

The beast felt its flesh lift off of its bones. Above, Suction was spinning and spinning. The mastodon fired another tusk, the bone sticking the monster through its other flap. Suction flailed and crashed yet again.

Crab's pincer came out of nowhere and pinched off a long strip of flesh along its chest. The mastodon whipped around and donkey-kicked Crab in its solar plexus. Crab was thrown so high up in the air that when it landed, several bones had shattered inside its body.

Fireball remained hovering in the sky. The dragon monster was a spectator enjoying the show. Its cunning, devious smile liked what it was seeing, and that was fresh mastodon blood. Just for fun, the hovering beast spit a line of fire all around the mastodon so it couldn't avoid another bite attack from Centipede. From its tail to head, more bites oozed blood. Mega Mastodon wheeled in agony. The challenger threw its body forward and took a chunk out of Centipede's side with its mouth, crushing shell, and spilling yellow guts, and bags of bile onto the ice.

Buying time to recover from its wounds, the mastodon took a giant bite out of the ice. It chewed up the ice into smaller bits and spit them out like glass with great force. Those shards stabbed Crab, halting the deadly threat from another offensive move.

Suction was airborne again, constantly dripping blood from the fresh hole in its flap. The mastodon took another mouthful of ice and spat it upwards. Suction absorbed the ice shards. Sharp little knives stabbed it internally. When Suction collapsed yet again, it would stay down for a time.

Mega Mastodon's moves didn't save it from damage.

New harm was coming.

Centipede crawled under its belly and bored another onslaught of tiny holes, many of them around its genitals. The beast stumbled onto its side in super pain.

Fireball, ready to take advantage of a weakened opponent, swooped down. Fireball used its back legs to pick up Mega Mastodon by its front legs. The dragon sprung up to the sky and dropped the mastodon down from hundreds of feet.

The collision caused chunks of ice to burst underneath Mega Mastodon. Writhing in pain, it struggled to turn off of its back and get up. It wailed, suffering the effect of many shattered vertebrae. Through wild conflagrations of awesome pain, the mastodon managed to turn right side up again. It bled from top to bottom. One leg was on the verge of buckling.

Across from where the mastodon stood, the villains were coming for another contest.

This time, the mastodon would be nothing against their power.

WATCH THEM KILL

The fourth rocket was loaded into the firing box. Everybody struggled to put out more effort. Monica's arms and back suffered from lugging the impossibly heavy loads. She didn't complain. Nobody did. This final showdown would make or break the world. There wasn't time for complaining.

"You see that?" Brian said. "Mastodon's not doing so well. They're about to kill him."

"Then our timing is about right," Tank added. "Help me load the final rocket. He did right by us. Now we have to do right by the world. This is the home stretch. Make or break. Move it."

Shrieks of the mastodon repeated. Judging by the disparity of its cries, the beast knew its death was incoming. She couldn't help but look as long as possible.

The four monsters charged at the near-death hero.

Monica couldn't stand to watch without helping it fight. "Come on. Do something. Save yourself."

"Your sentiments are touching," Brian said. "But The Tank's right. No matter who wins, we lose. Now help us load this thing."

"Let them kill each other," The Tank barked. "Whoever's left...I'm taking them out. We'll be heroes. Just think. We'll be on T-shirts."

Monica rolled her eyes. "There's something seriously wrong with you."

"Yeah," The Tank agreed. "I'm freezing my ass off and praying a monster doesn't eat me. Obviously something's wrong with me."

Monica turned away from the battle. "Shut up. Fine. Let's load her up."

She knew this was Mega Mastodon's final moment.

The second she stopped watching, everything changed.
The mastodon wasn't done fighting.

STOMP

Shadows eclipsed Mega Mastodon's body. He was being flanked from every direction so there would be nowhere for it to run. The monsters hovered around him, knowing they had the upper hand. Centipede's legs wriggled as the mouths on the underside of its body licked their chops. Crab was test pinching the air. Suction had suffered the most damage. Its spin was slower, and its body was lopsided. It took longer to gain enough air to create a significant suction, but give it another few minutes, and it would reach full killing capacity. Fireball remained confident and poised in the air. Once Mega Mastodon was finished, it could reign supreme unchallenged.

Through reptilian thought processes, Fireball imagined humans running from its hot flames. Then it would touch down and gobble up body after body. No matter how insane its hunger became, Fireball would always be fed. Every day would be a gluttonous buffet.

Before the four could swoop down and pick to pieces their enemy, they were thrown backwards. All four dodged Mega Mastodon when it sprang up from its weak position. Using every ounce of power remaining in its body, the mastodon bent all four legs in mid-air. When it landed, a great big STOMP rocked the earth. The reverberations channeled deep into the ground. Along the extensive battlefield, parts of the earth crumbled. New crevasses forked the ground. Pitfalls and rifts opened. The earth was rearranged by the power of the mastodon's stomp.

When the rumbles calmed into silence, Mega Mastodon lay dead.

All four of its legs were broken.

Fireball was about to swoop down and eat its enemy's carcass when all hell broke out.

UNLEASHED

The three of them had loaded the final rocket. The Tank was about to start the truck when everybody was knocked on their asses by the earth's shifting. Monica was spread out on the ice, trying her best to recover. She stayed down. The rumbles, shifts, and collapsing pockets of the ground beneath them continued for at least another ten minutes. She pictured dynamite being blasted from underground. New hills, plateaus, and drops were created in the crumbling landscape. Mega Mastodon had jumped so high and had come down so hard to cause all of this chaos. Once everything settled, she noticed the mastodon didn't get up. It lay bleeding and dead on the ice.

"What was the point of that?" The Tank asked them. "It jumped up in the air, knocked us on our asses, and now the ground's all fucked up. What does that do? I picture a kid throwing a tantrum. Not a warrior making a final stand."

Brian's lips were trembling.

He stared on at the landscape visibly shaken.

"Brian, are you okay?" Monica touched his shoulder. The man gave a startle. "What's going on?"

"That wasn't throwing a tantrum. That was sending out an S.O.S."

"Huh?" Tank was confused. "I don't understand."

Brian turned to Monica. "Randall Sterling was onto something big. His theory about the shifting and dumping of life forms here in the ice millions of years ago...I think his theory is about to be proven correct.

"You said an electrical current brought those cavemen to life, and those mastodons. It makes me wonder, what else was brought back to life?"

191

Up from the rearranged landscape, that question was answered.

THE FINAL FRONT

Monica had to collect every ounce of sanity left in her being to properly take in the next spectacular moments. She stood with the other two people trying to ingest the proceedings. Climbing from the ice, new beasts presented themselves. Answering Mega Mastodon's call, Monica mentally catalogued them.

From one side of the broken battlefield, it appeared. She imagined a giant deer combined with a Yeti creature. Dubbing it Wendigo, the beast towered as tall as half a skyscraper. The giant horns were long and tipped with many sharp edges. Its eyes glowed a neon blue. White jowls oozed frothy saliva. Its bony body bragged of hunger and its eagerness to feed.

Triple a normal bear's size, a collection of thirty polar bears crawled free. Their bodies weighed a ton a piece. Scraggly coats of white hair covered powerhouse bodies. Enormous claws could be seen extending from their paws.

Another fleet of challengers came next. Glyptodons, the size of Mac trucks, were charging forth. They mimicked enormous, gray-armored armadillos. Their tails had thick clubs on the end. They swung them at the air, bragging damage to any enemy.

Hybrid Stegosauruses covered in plated armor much thicker than their known ancestors rose up, giving numbers to the already large front of challengers.

The strangest sight yet was the T-rex whose body was pure white with bright blue eyes. Monica dubbed it Winter Rex. The giant stomped onto the fighting platform ready to destroy.

The beasts did what nature told them to do.

Fight to the death.

The Tank pulled her away from observing the scene. "Get in the vehicle. I'm about to use my toy to kill 'em all."

Monica rushed into the vehicle. Before Brian could take cover, a giant shard of ice pierced him through the middle. He was killed instantly, stuck through with the frozen sharp pole.

"Jesus! Brian!" Monica couldn't do anything to help him. "How many more people have to die before this is over?"

"Hopefully he'll be the last." When The Tank turned on the ignition, it wouldn't kick over. "Shit! The cold must be getting to the engine. I'll keep trying."

While The Tank kept trying the engine, the battle only grew bloodier.

Winter Rex was wrestling with Centipede. Centipede had wrapped around its midsection and was chewing through its reptilian skin. Tracks of blood and burbling red wounds covered Rex. Its short arms couldn't reach to rip off the ever-moving centipede.

Winter Rex roared with anger and pain as more of its blood was shed. It finally smartened up by jumping high in the air and landing hard on its back. The landing smashed centipede. Centipede broke off into six different segments. Trying to escape, the collection of polar bears played various games of tug-of-war, like centipede leg rip and beat the insect, until Centipede was nothing but piping hot yellow guts on the ice.

Suction went on the offensive by spinning above the polar bears. Its sucking force lifted the polar bears off of the ground. Lifting them into its gummy maw, Suction acted like a paper shredder and reduced the bears into dead strips and pieces to be digested and excreted.

Wendigo charged Crab with its long and sharp antlers. Its antlers pierced into Crab's midsection. Green blood gushed, giving advance warning of the great heap of guts that slopped free. Pounding those antlers again and again, the crab's torso turned into an empty crater. Crab's two pincers clipped off Wendigo's head in one last act of life.

The army of Stegosauruses was bathed in a twenty fireball offensive. Each ball was hot enough to instantly incinerate the prehistoric challengers. The Glyptodons were next. Fireball used one giant sub-atomic ball the size of its body to reduce the giant plated armadillos into bright blazing charcoal briquettes. The fire literally melted skin, muscle, and changed bone into black ash.

Winter Rex was the last challenger alive. The raging, growling, hungry dinosaur raced up to Suction, champed its giant mouth upwards, and chewed the manta ray spinning disc into four pieces. Each bleeding section slapped the ice in twitching, bleeding-out piles. Winter Rex stomped those pieces into ketchup-packet debris.

Fireball touched down opposite Winter Rex. The fighters stared each other down. Sizing one another up. Deciding how to dispatch their enemy. The stretch of silence extended for so long, Monica wondered if the beasts were going to attack each other at all.

Winter Rex shrieked, showing a purple mouth with a thick red tongue. Those long, hideous teeth were ready to stick and rip. Vaulting forward, the dinosaur rushed full speed to conquer its enemy. Fireball didn't advance. It stood there in wait. Once Winter Rex was close enough, Fireball spread out its wings and wrapped them around the dinosaur. The dragon took flight, clutching the dinosaur up against its body.

Fireball was taking head butt after head butt to the face. Blood burbled from its nostrils and its left eye was half-squashed. Still, the dragon flew higher. Winter Rex reared back to take a bite out of Fireball's face when the dragon clenched its wings so hard, it broke Winter Rex's spine. Fireball dropped the dead dinosaur from nine hundred feet. When the dinosaur struck down, it lay there a crumpled, dead mess.

"Well, they didn't last long," Monica griped. "What do we do now?"

The Tank kept cussing under his breath to get his vehicle working.

Mega Mastodon's avengers were slain.

Fireball remained alive and angrier than before.

He kept trying the ignition.

Fireball sucked in a breath and prepared to incinerate them.

GUT CHECK

"Come on you, bitch. Am I not pressing your buttons right? You showing off for the passenger, huh? You only like to argue with me when the shit hits the fan. Is that it?"

Fireball widened its jaw. Its neck bulged with a great gathering ball of flames.

"We're about to be cooked crispy," Monica said. "Is this billion dollar piece of shit supposed to work, or what? Do you know what's at stake here?"

"I do! The human race. Global extinction. And my neck paycheck!"

The creature stepped into a dip on the treacherous ice terrain and lost its footing. That misstep bought them precious moments.

The Tank remained determined to win the battle. "She used a lot of power firing those missiles earlier. She's recharging her batteries. They're special batteries. The cold actually acts like a solar panel in a way. Instead of sunlight, the cold charges it up."

"I understand," Monica yelled. "You don't have to give me a lesson, teacher. I only want you to get it to work. Shoot the fucking thing out of existence, would you? You have any idea how many people have died tonight? I've seen so much blood."

"Okay, baby," The Tank said to his vehicle, talking smooth. "I'm going to ask you one more time. Start for me, huh? I'll take you out for a nice date. I'll spend top dollar to wine and dine you, honey. I'll treat you really nice."

"Quit talking like that, you weirdo! Get a girlfriend. And get this thing started!"

Fireball stood up on its back legs. It stretched out its wings to show off its enormity. Small tendrils of fire spooled out of its nostrils holes. From the pit of its throat, an orange glow grew brighter as the birth of another ball of fire was imminent.

The engine kicked over.

The Tank had five seconds to save them from being cooked crispy. His hand was quick to work the internal computer. "Sights locked on target. Rockets are launched!"

Soooooooooooonk!

Soooooooooooonk!

Soooooooooooonk!

Soooooooooooonk!

Soooooooooooonk!

Five rockets shot right at Fireball. When they made contact, Fireball's stomach opened wide. The sideways slit ate the rockets. The torso mouth closed. Monica could hear the muffled explosion of each rocket.

Fireball stood there unaffected.

The Tank stared on at the beast in total concentration.

His weapon had failed.

FINAL MOMENT

"We could run," Monica suggested, "but we're out in the middle of long stretch of nothing. That thing would chase us down and cook us the same. I guess this is it? Humanity loses."

"Wrong," The Tank said, suddenly smiling. "I'm glad that creature ate them up. It'll concentrate the power of my missiles. Watch me douse Fireball's internal flame. Five...four...three...two...ONE!"

Monica wasn't sure what she was supposed to be seeing. She sat rigidly in the seat awaiting a result. Her eyes watched. The ability to take it in was on a several second delay. Monica's eyes only got wider when it finally happened.

Fireball was towering over them one moment, about to take flight and dump a shower of fireballs upon them, when from its belly, a spinning tornado of motion burst free. The impact was so powerful, Fireball's arms, legs, head, and tail were ripped from its spine. Guts were spinning in the visual air blender. The tornado was now one of pure gore.

The Tank drove the vehicle away from the tornado. He drove his hybrid tank/Hummer back towards the university. Before the tornado died out, a single talon from Fireball's body smashed through the windshield and stabbed the driver in the throat.

The Tank was instantly dead. His head was connected to his body only by the thinnest pink thread. His arms and legs did death jitters. The vehicle was stopped. The tornado was still headed in her direction. Monica didn't know how much time the cycle of air had remaining before it dissipated.

She couldn't push Tank out of the driver's seat. She wasn't strong enough. She didn't have enough time to do anything else but retreat. Running up the hill towards the university, she dodged shards of Fireball's broken-up bones. They punctured the earth, jutting up like anatomical sculptures. A giant spine flailed in the air until it was thrown at the university building. Lashing like a whip, the bone caused half the brick and concrete structure to implode. The dragon skull struck the parking lot, erupting into thousands of porcelain pieces. Monica ducked and covered. She couldn't run anymore. Every ounce of energy was used up in retreating from the strangest tornado in history.

The night's cold was sucking what she would've had remaining to keep moving. She stayed on her side, catching her breath, and crying. Images of the people she met in a flash living and dying haunted her. The inklings of dawn on the sky broke her free from her thoughts. Fireball was dead. She was alive. The tornado had ended.

The ordeal was over.

Or so she wanted to believe.

EPILOGUE: AMERICA'S NEW POLICY

A chopper touched down on the parking lot. Men dressed in black military garb searched the area. Soon, they approached her. They helped her up off of the ground and ushered her into the chopper. When they took flight, a military man was shining a light into her eyes and asking her questions. "What is your name? Where are you? Did you sustain any injuries? What do you remember about the last few hours?"

Monica answered the questions. She peered out through the window at the battle-torn town. She couldn't believe the ordeal had ended, and she survived.

The chopper flew to a temporary military base outside of town. The group had taken over a community center. Survivors were being treated for their wounds. She didn't stay there long. Monica was delivered to yet another helicopter that transported her to an airport. A single engine plane flew her to an unnamed private island on the Pacific Ocean.

The island was covered in dense trees. She saw a waterfall cascade down a rock face. Everything else was the endless greenery of trees. Military escorted her into an underground bunker. The bunker was surrounded by high fences topped with rearms of barbed wire. She thought of a high-security prison. The area was cut out of the wild. She couldn't figure out what this place was or why she was here.

Her thoughts went to the worst possible outcome.

This is top-secret government stuff. You saw Fireball up close and personal. You know too much. They want to bury you under the system. I'll never see my parents again.

Monica walked down a short flight of stairs. She moved through five different security checkpoints before reaching what resembled a boardroom with a long table at the center of the room. Military men with M-16s stood watching the meeting. Thirty persons were seated at the table. They were a mix of military and civilians. The set of military personnel who had delivered her here asked her to sit in an empty seat. She followed orders without resistance.

Curiosity welled inside of her.

What kind of a meeting was she attending? Why did she have to be here? She was Monica Lake. Ex-con. A security worker who survived hell. She felt ill-equipped to attend what was obviously a secret government meeting.

The hard-faced man at the head of the table introduced himself as Colonel Pershing.

"I'm going to get right to it. Our world has survived hell. America has changed its policy towards any invader or enemy threat. We kill it, and we kill it with extreme prejudice. Executive orders are being written and signed as we speak to support our president's stance on enemy invaders.

"So what the hell are you doing here on this cast off forsaken island? They didn't even name this island. It's only a number. The existence of this place is unknown to the public. The best way to describe the purpose of this island is to say this. Imagine what's hidden under our feet as a Guantanamo Bay for monsters."

Awe swept the room. Some scrunched their brows in disbelief. Nobody thought the colonel was lying about the monsters. After Fireball's attacks, the world knew these creatures existed.

"Our government has stored hundreds of years' worth of beasts, aquatic monsters, random misfires of creation, and things that even H.P. Lovecraft didn't have the imagination to put into his books. Below us is where nightmare creatures have been kept under lock and key.

"The moment Fireball was declared dead, the president signed a new order. He wants everything under our feet exterminated. We're cleaning house, people. We could nuke the island and wash our hands of this mess. The problem is, nuclear technology strengthened Fireball. We learned our lesson. No nukes. We take no chances.

"Another problem with dropping a bomb on this place, we have security below who haven't reported in for forty-eight hours. The place was put on lockdown by somebody below. We're going to have to bypass security just to get into the prison. We want to check for survivors, and during the rescue mission, we blow to smithereens anything squirming, writhing, moving, or trying to bite us. The prime directive is simple. Search and rescue. Kill and destroy.

"Everybody in this room is the most qualified to dispatch this unusual batch of enemies. Your country needs you. I want you on my team. There's no great sum of money or high honor for serving your country. Everything here is classified. What I can offer you is a job for the rest of your lives with great benefits. Most of all, you'll be serving your country in the most honorable way. You're the best of the best. What say you? Will you join me in turning the prison below us into a monster killing box?"

The table erupted in enthused responses.

They were on board.

Monica thought about her life. Being an honor student. Going to jail wrongly for drug charges. Being sent to Alaska under false pretenses. Then surviving Fireball and everything connected to the beast's attacks. She was meant to do ultimate good in the world. The chance to prove herself arrived in a very strange package.

She accepted her fate.

Monica stood up and pounded her fist against the table. "Enough talk. Let's kill some fucking monsters!"

The colonel smiled at her.

"Okay. That's what I like to hear. *We'll get started right away*."

THE END

CHECK OUT OTHER GREAT KAIJU NOVELS

KAIJU WINTER
by **Jake Bible**

The Yellowstone super volcano has begun to erupt, sending North America into chaos and the rest of the world into panic. People are dangerous and desperate to escape the oncoming mega-eruption, knowing it will plunge the continent, and the world, into a perpetual ashen winter. But no matter how ready humanity is, nothing can prepare them for what comes out of the ash: Kaiju!

RAIJU
by **K.H. Koehler**

His home destroyed by a rampaging kaiju, Kevin Takahashi and his father relocate to New York City where Kevin hopes the nightmare is over. Soon after his arrival in the Big Apple, a new kaiju emerges. Qilin is so powerful that even the U.S. Military may be unable to contain or destroy the monster. But Kevin is more than a ragged refugee from the now defunct city of San Francisco. He's also a Keeper who can summon ancient, demonic god-beasts to do battle for him, and his creature to call is Raiju, the oldest of the ancient Kami. Kevin has only a short time to save the city of New York. Because Raiju and Qilin are about to clash, and after the dust settles, there may be no home left for any of them!

CHECK OUT OTHER GREAT KAIJU NOVELS

MURDER WORLD | KAIJU DAWN
by Jason Cordova
& Eric S Brown

Captain Vincente Huerta and the crew of the Fancy have been hired to retrieve a valuable item from a downed research vessel at the edge of the enemy's space.
It was going to be an easy payday.
But what Captain Huerta and the men, women and alien under his command didn't know was that they were being sent to the most dangerous planet in the galaxy.
Something large, ancient and most assuredly evil resides on the planet of Gorgon IV. Something so terrifying that man could barely fathom it with his puny mind. Captain Huerta must use every trick in the book, and possibly write an entirely new one, if he wants to escape Murder World.

KAIJU ARMAGEDDON
by Eric S. Brown

The attacks began without warning. Civilian and Military vessels alike simply vanished upon the waves. Crypto-zoologist Jerry Bryson found himself swept up into the chaos as the world discovered that the legendary beasts known as Kaiju are very real. Armies of the great beasts arose from the oceans and burrowed their way free of the Earth to declare war upon mankind. Now Dr. Bryson may be the human race's last hope in stopping the Kaiju from bringing civilization to its knees.
This is not some far distant future. This is not some alien world. This is the Earth, here and now, as we know it today, faced with the greatest threat its ever known. The Kaiju Armageddon has begun.

CHECK OUT OTHER GREAT KAIJU NOVELS

ATOMIC REX
by Matthew Dennion

The war is over, humanity has lost, and the Kaiju rule the earth.

Three years have passed since the US government attempted to use giant mechs to fight off an incursion of kaiju. The eight most powerful kaiju have carved up North America into their respective territories and their mutant offspring also roam the continent. The remnants of humanity are gathered in a remote settlement with Steel Samurai, the last of the remaining mechs, as their only protection. The mech is piloted by Captain Chris Myers who realizes that humanity will not survive if they stay at the settlement. In order to preserve the human race, he leaves the settlement unprotected as he engages on a desperate plan to draw the eight kaiju into each other's territories. His hope is that the kaiju will destroy each other. Chris will encounter horrors including the amorphous Amebos, Tortiraus the Giant turtle , and the nuclear powered mutant dinosaur Atomic Rex!

KAIJU DEADFALL
by JE Gurley

Death from space. The first meteor landed in the Pacific Ocean near San Francisco, causing an earthquake and a tsunami. The second wiped out a small Indiana city. The third struck the deserts of Nevada. When gigantic monsters- Ishom, Girra, and Nusku- emerge from the impact craters, the world faces a threat unlike any it had ever known - Kaiju . NASA catastrophist Gate Rutherford and Special Ops Captain Aiden Walker must find a way to stop the creatures before they destroy every major city in America..

CHECK OUT OTHER GREAT KAIJU NOVELS

KAIJU SPAWN
by David Robbins
& Eric S Brown

Wally didn't believe it was really the end of the world until he saw the Kaiju with his own eyes. The great beasts rose from the Earth's oceans, laying waste to civilization. Now Wally must fight his way across the Kaiju ravaged wasteland of modern day America in search of his daughter. He is the only hope she has left . . . and the clock is ticking.

From authors David Robbins (Endworld) and Eric S Brown (Kaiju Apocalypse), Kaiju Spawn is an action packed, horror tale of desperate determination and the battle to overcome impossible odds.

KUA MAU
by Mark Onspaugh

The Spider Islands. A mysterious ship has completed a treacherous journey to this hidden island chain. Their mission: to capture the legendary monster, Kua'Mau. Thinking they are successful, they sail back to the United States, where the terrifying creature will be displayed at a new luxury casino in Las Vegas. But the crew has made a horrible mistake - they did not trap Kua'Mau, they took her offspring. Now hot on their heels comes a living nightmare, a two hundred foot, one hundred ton tentacled horror, Kua'Mau, Kaiju Mother of Wrath, who will stop at nothing to safeguard her young. As she tears across California heading towards Vegas, she leaves a monumental body-count in her wake, and not even the U. S. military or private black ops can stop this city-crushing, havoc-wreaking monstrous mother of all Kaiju as she seeks her revenge.

www.ingramcontent.com/pod-product-compliance
Lightning Source LLC
Chambersburg PA
CBHW020752210626
46807CB00018B/2532